The Farm Homecoming

BY

Deana Rae Higgins

ISBN 978-0-6151-4923-3

"Want to play baby, you know I really think that's what you need, a good beating to put you in place, like a junk yard dog, you need to know just who, is master here, understand baby, me, got that."

He grabbed my head leaning in for another kiss, this time I met him coming up, like I wanted to kiss him back, I bit down hard on his lip and held on, I felt my teeth go all the way thru his lip and this time, I tasted his blood. He head butted me, and I let go, I felt so dazed I had to close my eyes to steady myself, my head hurt so bad I couldn't think and every time I tried to move I wanted to throw up, when at last I opened my eyes, I could hardly see, there was blood running down my face in a steady stream across my eyes. I could hear Jason laughing, loud, and the room seemed to be moving with every laugh he made. I felt my clothes ripped from my body, like I was a rag doll, and then I was nude. I tried to move, sense Jason had gotten off my legs to rip my clothes off, but I couldn't, my legs didn't seem to hear me.

"Please."

I started to beg but Jason put his hand over my mouth to shut me up, and with on quick movement he was on top again, this time he had spread my legs wide and climbed on top of me, entering me with a hard force that ripped me open to him. He started kissing me and I tried to stop him and again he hit me full force in the face with his fist, chipping my front tooth.

Dear Reader's,

My name is Cara-Ann; this is a story about the farm I grew up on. It's about murder, rape, secret's and coming home.

Secrets of rape should never be kept to yourself, tell someone and if they won't or don't care, tell someone until you find someone who does. Survival is the end goal.

Please read my story of survival...

In love,
Cara-Ann Raye

FOR:

My GRANDCHILDREN

Arthur, Stephen, Christian, Anastasia, Elisha, Eli, Kristopher, William, Bowen, Dylan, Dominic, and Alexzander

11 grandsons and 1 granddaughter

“The Homecoming”
By Deana Rae Higgins

Table of contents:

Chapter 01
"The Homecoming"
By Deana Rae Higgins

Coming home

The sun was shinning bright, so bright in fact, I couldn't see. I looked, with my hand shielding my eyes, past the train and the people getting off. But I couldn't see my ride. I had worn my favorite pant suit, a soft green, so standing in the dust and dirt didn't set well with me, I had talked to mother that morning, had they forgotten me, I wondered, and then behind me, a soft whisper, of my name.

"Cara-Ann."

I turned to meet the most beautiful green eyes, he was six foot easy, and blond, a stranger to me, yet he knew my name.

"Do you know me?" I asked, sharply, annoyed from waiting in the heat and dust from the train.

"I was sent by your mother to pick you up, my name is Jack, I work for your parents. Do you have luggage? My car is over here."

As I stood there staring at Jack, wondering what he did for my parents, my mouth speechless, for once, I could only shake my head and reach into my travel bag for my baggage slip, holding it out, like a defiant child, caught, red-handed, with cookie in hand.

Jack, looked at my face, and hand, grabbing the ticket, with a shrug, turned and walked off. Seconds later he was back, with my luggage in hand, making my heavy suitcase look small and light. He walked past me with a simple nod, walking to a small car, throwing my cases in the back, and opening the driver's door, sliding in and starting the car, in one quick movement.

As I stood, there, watching him walk away, my mind clearing and registering what was going on, I realized I best hurry, he had backed up the car and was staring at me.

"Not a gentleman, I see." I mumbled under my breath as I opened the door to get in.

"Nope, never been accused of that, miss, best buckle up, don't want to get stopped for no seatbelt."

As he took off in a whirl of speed and dust, I grabbed

the belt and belted it, catching my breath. Questions began to pour out of my mouth, as fast as I could get them out.

"Is my dad ok? What do you do for my parents? Do you live at the farm? What is going on with the farm?"

But without a word, Jack reached for the radio and turned it up, shutting me up. I could tell my face had turned bright red from being angry, so I turned and looked out the window, thinking to my self, we'll just see who has the last laugh when he's fired from his job.

The ride took forty-five minutes to get to the farm, I hadn't been home, sense I left for the big city, as dad called it. The road was dusty, I tried to roll the window up but it wouldn't work, allowing the dust to roll in coating everything with dust. As we turned off the main road I understood why, the fields were nothing but dirt and dust blowing in the wind.

The weather was mild and cool, perfect for a long drive, if I had a better driver, I thought, careful not to look at him.

As we approached the turnoff, I noticed that several fence's looked new, as least he works, my mind thought.

Seeing the house, made me gasp, the paint was pealing, the windows looked dirty, almost as if it was empty. There was no grass just dirt and dust all around the house.

As I turned to ask what had happened, Jack stopped the car suddenly and jumped out before I could get the words out. He threw my luggage on the driveway and jumped in and took off, without a word. Leaving me standing alone outside in the dust.

"What a jerk." was all I could spit out as he drove away. Grabbing my heavy bag's, dragging them up the stairs, to the door, helped release some of my anger, worry had taken its place.

I started thinking of how beautiful the house had been when I was young. The bar-be-que's, the party's, the family gatherings, the birthday parties, the many Christmas' with the family and friends from town. What happened and why wasn't I told?

As I opened the door, a strange odor escaped, a mixture of dust, dirt and sickness, now I was really worried. My mother always kept her home in order, was she sick, I had came home to help with my father's illness, mother had said nothing about herself. Where was the help?

As I looked around, I worried where everyone was? I set my bags down, to tired to carry upstairs now, I started to look for my parents. The kitchen I found was clean, but in need of repairs and paint, and looked nothing like the kitchen of my childhood, there was no fresh baked smell, no garden fresh vegetables on the counters, and no canned goods filling the shelves.

I went up the back stairs, they seemed to have been cleaned, and was well lit, my father had put them in for my mother, close to the kitchen and bedrooms upstairs, the house had been my grandparents, my father had grown up in this home, they had added a formal sitting room downstairs and library upstairs, off the main stairs when my parents first married, it was fun as children for James, my brother and I to run up and down the stairs, a big huge wide old staircase, like you see in the pictures of old southern homes.

Once James slid down the rail hitting the bottom so hard he broke his arm in three places, after that, the stairway was off limits, but we never listened.

As I got to the top of the small back stairway, the first room was my old bedroom; the door stood open, waiting for my return.

My bed was made and the room fairly clean. It was still painted a soft green, faded with time and the curtains, washed and cleaned matched the bed sheets and bedspread to a tee, picked by me, made by my mother. Most of my stuff was packed away, I saw, in boxes, in the closet, my porcelain dolls I collected as a teenager, dozens, with long locks of curled hair and fancy dress‘ stood in glass box‘s around the room, dad had made each glass box, to fit each doll and her dress.

"You can unpack what you want, I left the dolls out, just couldn‘t pack away such beautiful things, your dad enjoyed making those box‘s as much as you enjoyed having them, just seemed a shame not to see them."

I turned to see my mother, older but still a beauty, I saw. She looked tired but well.

I ran to her, hugging her, tears streaming down my face. She held me, for what seemed like hours.

“I’m glad your home” She spoke at last, patting my back.

“Oh mama, what happened? The house? Is daddy ok? Questions poured out.

“Calm down Cara-Ann, first, your father, he’s sleeping, come lets check on him, then we’ll go have tea. He’s got his good days and bad ones, but over all he’s the same, just weaker. He sleep’s a lot and it’s for the best, the doctor said, it could be a week or a month, you know your father, he never goes by any ones rules but his own.

As she talked we walked to the end of the hallway, to my parents room. I worried why they hadn’t moved closer to the kitchen, to mine or my brother’s room. My face must have said what I was thinking.

“I wanted to change bedrooms but your father wouldn’t hear of it.

We stopped at the door, it was closed, I reached for the doorknob to open the door, but mama touched my hand.

“Don’t wake him and don’t expect him to be the father he was.” was all she whispered as she withdrew her hand.

I opened the door; the room was dark, except for a small dim lamp next to the bed. My father could be heard, a soft whistling sound as he took each breath.

As I approached the bed, I saw his face, white, thin and very old looking; he looked more dead then alive. I leaned down and kissed the top of his white hair, still full and thick.

My mother had stopped at the door and waited, now she hand signaled me with a snap of her fingers, to follow her out, I did so without a glance back, softly closing the door behind me.

She turned and walked to the stairs, walking down them without a word said between us.

When we reached the kitchen, I sat down at the table, knowing my mother wouldn't want help, I watched as she put the water on, filling the kettle, and lighting the fire. We tried to buy her a new stove for Christmas one year, but she wouldn't hear of it.

She then gathered the box of tea bags and honey from the countertop, sitting them on the table. Then she gathered two cups and spoons, plastic from a drawer, never use metal in tea or coffee, grandma always said. She grabbed the hot water kettle and a dish rag, and sat both herself and the kettle on the rag at the same time.

Remembering the cake, she jumped up and moved about getting the plates and forks, before setting down again, this time with a sigh.

Cara-Ann watched without a word, as her mother moved about, not talking.

When at last her mother had sighed, she poured the water, while her mother cut the cake. It was chocolate; Cara-Ann's favorite, and freshly baked.

When at last the tea bags had been deposited into cups, honey poured and cake on white porcelain plates, given to her mother on the day she married her father, by her grandmother, mother begun to tell her story of sorrow, Cara-Ann spell bound by the sound of her mothers soft voice and the story she told, listened in awe.

"It started, right after Christmas last year, when you and your brother came to visit; your father was well then, and so full of life. He loved having you and your brother home, we so missed you both."

"Mom." was all I got out, as she held up her hand, to silence me, as she continued with her story, stopping only to drink from her tea cup, leaving her cake untouched.

Cara-Ann however, savored every bite of hers, before she even touched her tea, before her mother had gotten very far in her story, making her mother laugh as she watched her eat.

"The town decided they wanted to widen the road thru town, in case the highway comes thru here. Like that will happen, not in this back woods, run down town." Her mothers voice raising ever so slightly as she spoke, then stopping and regaining her composure.

"They sent a letter in the mail, with an offer to buy a hundred acre's on the north side of the ranch, your father laughed so hard, I though he had gone mad.

He showed me the letter with the offer, and I too laughed so hard, tears ran down my cheek. We didn't take it as serious; I threw it away in the trash and forgot all about it.

Then about a week later a check for the low price offered came in the mail. Your dad called and talked to someone, who said, to come in, next town hall meeting and bring it with us. So we did, only it was too late.

Somehow they had taken our land for pennies on the dollar for what it was worth, and we had no say, except thru the courts, so we hired a lawyer. He costs us more then the land was worth, but your father wouldn't let it go.

We took it all the way to the country court house over in Hinesburg, and you know how your father fells about going there.

It took six months to get on the docket there and when we did go to court, we lost.

They said, the city had a right to our land, for what ever price they wanted to pay us, and they took out their lawyer's charge and court costs.

The check in the end was two dollars and ten cents; our lawyer was thirty-five thousand. All our savings."

At this point, I could only stare at my empty cup, my mother poured more water for us both, adding honey and stirring before she continued her story.

I could only do the same, my mind running eighty miles a minute thinking about, everything she had said, as I stirred my tea.

When at last mother began to talk, her voice cracked, causing me to look up, to see a single tear roll off her cheek.

"Your father was so hurt; you know all his friends run that city hall, down there in town. Kids he grew up with, buddies he played pool with and drank beer with, he was even godfather to a couple of their kids.

Them good for nothing assholes, never did like them. Sorry, didn't mean to cuss, thank goodness your father didn't hear. He trusted them fools right up to the end, still thinks, there under a voo do spell or something."

Laughing at this point, she stopped to catch her breath and take a sip off tea to calm her nerves.

"He, your father, tried to call them, but they, them big shots, over at city hall, wouldn't take his calls or call back.

Finally, he got tired of asking and went to town, by himself, without me, or without even telling me, I didn't know where he was, I kept calling his cell phone, but it kept going straight to voice mail. I thought it was the phone, you know how our reception is out here, half the time it works and the other half its useless, waste of money, I say, but that was your fathers doing, case I needed him, he said. What a laugh, couldn't even get him.

Three hours later, Midge, my friend, at the hospital, you remember her, well she called said that your father had been brought in and could I bring in the insurance card, now she knew we didn't have insurance, I asked her later, and she said her boss was standing there and wanted to know if he had insurance before they admitted him into the hospital or sent him over to the county hospital.

So I drove there knowing once I got there if I didn't have money, he was out the door. I stopped at the bank, got what was left in our checking and savings and got your grandmas jewelry out of our safety deposit box at the bank. I then headed over to the pawn shop and pawned the jewelry first.

I thought if I could get enough, they would keep him here. Cash is cash in hand. When I got to the hospital, I knew it was bad, the way they were looking at me, as I walked in.

Soon as I told them we had no insurance, and only ten grand in hand, all hell broke loose. That little girl at the desk was up and in the emergency room quick, with that news.

They packed him up and had him sent to county, before they even told me, and charged us five grand, for his little visit. They didn't even tell me what was wrong, till I got to county.

Your father had a stroke, while at city hall, yelling at them fools. By the time he was taken care, it was too late, the damage was done, it's hard for him to speak or move and he may never get better.

His doctor's bills and hospital bills cleaned out us and what I got from selling most the land. All that's left is this part, with the house on it and the road into here and the county gets that when your father dies, for his medical bills. Jack, the young man you met, he helps out some with things, I clean his house and do his laundry, once a week, when the nurse comes to visit, that's all the help, they'll give us.

Had to apply for food stamps, just to eat, thank God,

your father doesn't know, and don't you say anything, you hear. "

I was so dazed; all I could do was nod my head yes as an answer to her.

"I know it's a lot to take in, and I'm sorry I didn't call you. You don't have to worry; I'll get a small apartment in town, after your father…"

And then she began to cry, I moved my chair without lifting and held her as she cried. She cried big sobs of tears, never raising her voice loud, always remindful of my father sleeping upstairs. She cried until she had no more tears to cry, and then scolded herself for felling sorry for herself. I held her like a parent to a child, as she cried, thankful, I had come home

. When at last she fished, we held hands, just smiling at each other, and rocking back and forth very softly together.

Mother then stood up, said its time for bed, you must be tired, began to pick up the cups and plates, putting them in the sink, and turned to leave.

Turning off the light and turning on the hall light in one quick movement from years of living in the same home.

I couldn't believe that my parents home was gone, I wouldn't, I would do something, I told myself, as I followed mother up the stairs. At the top of the stairs she kissed my cheek, and with a wave, walked down to her room with my father, down the hall, just like a thousands times before, in my memories.

I turned as she shut the door behind her and entered the room of my childhood, turned the light on and shut the door.

I look around the room, robbed of every thing that was mine.

I walked over to the dresser and to my surprise, my childhood pajama's, worn a little big as a teenager, a perfect fit now, a nice long bath was in order.

Each room had its own bathroom; mine had been painted green, a soft mint green, with matching tile. The tub still had candles and bath salts from my youth, I was amazed, until I looked and saw they had new tags from the drugstore in town. Mother had remembered how much I loved them.

After a relaxing bath, I dug out some paper and pen to write down my plan to save my mothers home. I needed to see the papers from the court case. I was not a lawyer, but I knew a good one, next best thing. I was a graphic artist.

I started thinking about everything mother had said, I could not believe that the ranch had been taken over, that explained the new fences.

Then I stared thinking about the handy man Jack. What was his story? Why was he being so nice? What did he want in return? I didn't trust him. Yet, all I could think about was, how green his eyes were in the sunlight. My favorite color.

Sleep was what I needed.

Yet I awoke more tired then the night before. Dreams of

deceit, lies, highways that had gapping mouths, which laughed. Green eyes calling my name, whispered in the wind, ever so softly, making me strain my ears to hear it.

And most of all, I dreamed of death, our animals, my dad, my mom and my own. I cried out and woke myself, early, grateful to be free of my demon dreams. Yet, I also knew to take heed of my dreams, I had to be very careful and trust no one.

By the time mother had awoken at eight, coffee and hot rolls from the oven had been made and set on the table.

We drank hot coffee and ate sweet jelly from mother's garden on hot buttery made from scratch rolls.

We talked of early times, my brother and his family, old friends from school, but nothing from last night.

We laughed as if we had become school girls, on an sleep over, rotating between friends and parent and child.

When we had drank the pot of coffee and consumed way too many rolls with jelly, and our hearts were light and filled with love, did we come back to reality.

A sad trip back for us both. Mother rose, and quietly said, "I best see to your dad" and turned to leave. Before she reached the stairs, I asked, quickly.

"The lawyer's name and number, please mother?"

She turned, pointed to her desk, and softly spoke.

"His name is Michael Brown, office is in town, address on my desk, Cara-Ann, you watch your self, them boys in town, they don't care a thing for life.

You understand me child? This is not a game. I don't want to lose you too." She turned and headed upstairs, before I could respond to what she had said, but I took it to heart.

Time to clean up and head to town, and see what bees nest I can stir up. First stop, one Michael Brown, attorney at law, then city hall. It's been a while, but I think I can still remember my way around my hometown.

Welcome home Cara-Ann, no boring homecoming for you.

Chapter 02
"The Homecoming"
By Deana Rae Higgins

Remembering

Dragging my heavy suitcase's upstairs, at last, I started unpacking.

I had bought a new sun dress before I left; I laid it out, along with my makeup and hair products. I needed to look good, if I was going to get anything out of the lawyer or them old men at city hall.

I was glad I had taken the time to trim my hair before I had come home. It was a golden brown, and curled under, lying on top of my shoulders. It matched my light brown eyes. The dress a soft blue, hugged my curves, showing off my hard work at saying fit. When I was done, I stepped back from the mirror, took a good look at myself and decided that I looked pretty good.

Even thou I was tired and had bags under my eyes from not sleeping, the makeup and new dress did the job, I felt I could take on the world, I hoped I wouldn't have to. Grapping my purse I headed downstairs to the kitchen.

I found dad's truck keys on the peg beside the door, where they have hung for years. I hoped it was in good working condition.

The barn was behind the house, I opened the door expecting to see the truck rundown, but instead it looked good, and started right up. Someone had taken good care of it. Mother never learned to drive, never needed to, she said. Must have been Jack, I though.

I started off, down the drive, a little rusty at first, been a while since I had drove a stick shift, but like riding a bike, it comes back to you. I had stopped at the stop sign at the main road to town, waiting for the traffic to pass, when suddenly a new truck pulled in front of dad's truck, and stopped.

My heart began to race, I shoved the truck into reverse, ready to fee, when suddenly a man jumped out of the drivers side of the truck and started walking my way.

My heart froze, my breath gone, my lungs gasping for air as if the air had been sucked out of the world like a plastic bag, I stared in shook. I couldn't move, my heart was racing so fast, my whole world had turned upside down, my mind lost in time, I felt like, the world had stopped turning.

The air inside the truck felt hot. I felt hot. My lungs, no longer able to hold out, gasped, sucking in the hot air.

I rolled down the window, grateful for the cool air outside that came rushing in. My eyes never leaving the man walking up to my door, I looked him over from head to boot.

His black hair, so shiny, his brown eyes, still so puppy dogged, and as handsome as he was, in our youth. I remembered the first time I saw him, how so taken in I was by him. His smile, I noticed, still so very sexy. Somehow, after five years, Jason, my first love, still stopped me dead in my tracks.

"Hey sweetheart. How's my girl?" He yanked open my door and pulled me out and into his arms, in one quick movement, before I had a chance to catch hold of myself.

He smelled the same, a mixture of wood and musk, and a sweet sexy smell that always drove me crazy, and was working on me now.

His arms strong and hard, unlike the small youthful arms of childhood, held me tight, pulling me into a world of lust.

My body begin to relax and respond, bringing me out of my stupor.

I tried to push against his chest, but it too was strong and built nothing like his youth and all fetal attempts to release myself gone.

When at last he had hugged me for what seemed like forever, but really was only a second, he held me at arms length and looked at my eyes.

"You look good Cara-Ann, that big city agrees with you. You're staying, this time, right." And then he hugged me again. I couldn't find the words to say no, I wouldn't be staying, that as soon as I had helped my parents, I would escape to my home in the city, again, and again, from him.

Jason had been my first and only love so far. I had loved him so much.

We had gone together thru high school, all four years, Jason a year older, graduated before me.

My senior year without him scared me. I missed him so much and yet I had dreams that I wanted to accomplish. I didn't want to stay here and become a farmer's wife; I hated the farm and the country.

I wanted big cities and lots of people. Lots of new places and lots of adventure. But most of all I wanted a college degree and a great paying job, with children in the far future.

Jason didn't want any of that, he wanted a wife, kids and a farm, and I wondered if he found them.

"How did you know I was here?" I asked

"Your mom, told me last week. I came to visit and bring her some medicine for your father." laughing with his eyes.

"So where you headed pretty girl?" He asked as his eyes slid down my body and back to my eyes, making me blush.

"Town." Was all I could get out, knowing my face had turned red and he knew he had got to me, I started to jump back into the drivers seat, when he reached out and grabbed my arm, holding me softly.

"Cara-Ann don't get involved please, it's dangerous. I tired to help your parents but the town wouldn't let any of us help. It wasn't just them." He sighed out loud, before continuing.

"There where three farms. Widow Johnson's, the Dean's and yours. It was hard for us all to watch, but if the highway comes thru here, the town will need it, really. Cara-Ann, please."

I shook my arm loose, mad now, how dare he, hard to watch. What did his family lose? Was he in on it too, my mind reminded me, trust no one.

"My family, my problems, my business, now if you'll excuse me, I have work to do."

I jumped in the truck slamming the door, and started the truck, I had turned it off, when I saw Jason walk around his truck.

I rolled up the window and put the truck in gear. Jason, dumb founded, was still standing beside my door, sad looking and confused, shaking his head left to right, mouthing the words please, as I drove off, leaving him standing in the middle of the road.

My mind was fuming, how dare he. Just who did he think he was? Maybe the whole town was in on this movement, I would have to be very careful, they knew I was here, that's for sure. Sent out the big guns, ha, what a laugh. Damn girl; get a grip, it worked, almost.

You got over him a long time ago, I hope. It upset me that I let Jason unnerve me. So much time, so much has happened, last I heard he was dating Jill, my best friend from school.

I though about Jason, all the way to town, our first date, first kiss, our first time with each other. The good times, the laughs, the hurtful words, the black eye from his slapping me, when I told him, I was leaving town, to go to collage, how he had tried to controlled my friends even tried to stop me from leaving by giving my car four flat tires the day I left, but dad fixed them and warned me not to tell anyone my address and to get the hell out of dodge fast as I could.

.

"You'll pay Cara-Ann, you'll pay." Was this, what he was trying to tell me? At the time, it was just words of anger to me.

Was I wrong? Did he help to destroy my family for my leaving him? The boy I loved, who loved me, no way, but the man who he became, who learned to hate me for leaving him behind. Who knew? I would find out.

I'm a lot stronger then I was then, and I left him behind, forever.

He has no hold on me, I know, but his arms around me, holding me, attracting my senses. Was it just animal lust? It had to be, I'm sure of it. Or was I?

Town was small, one road in, and one out.

Off the main road, several dirt roads branched off to homes and the school. Main St was the only one paved. It didn't look much different then from childhood, except, in need of more repairs.

There were no new shops, in fact, several looked closed down. I passed the post office, on my right and stopped at the only red light in town. I looked around at the filthy streets and unkempt buildings.

To my surprise Jason was parked at the hardware store next to the bank, across from the post office, standing in back of his truck, arms crossed, smile wide, watching me.

I must tell him, I'm not interested, my mind said, my heart, wasn't telling yet.

What if Jason wasn't watching me because he still had a thing for me, but because he was told to watch me, for someone else for a whole different reason? Nope I didn't like it either way; it made chills run up and down my spine.

I turned away quick, pretending I didn't see him. As I drove off I looked in my rear view to see the smile leave his tan face, replaced with a frown.

The town city hall was at the end of town, or beginning, depending on which way you drove into town. House's on this side, looked freshly painted and well cared for, of course, I thought. City hall was in tip top shape and even the driveway had been paved.

The sign looked new and it looked like there were new windows too. So they had taken over the farm to make themselves look good. Now I was really mad.

I turned past city hall, leaving Jason staring at my dust, and pulled into the office of Michael Brown, attorney at law.

Mr. Brown's office was what used to be the Jenkins home. It was a small two bedroom, with a small fenced back yard.

Cara-Ann had spent a lot of time at this home, when she was younger and best friends with Jane Jenkins.

They had been best friends from the age of five, the first day of school, till the day she died.

The Jenkins family had gone to the rodeo in the next town, I was to go, but got sick, and had to stay home, on there way home, a drunk driver ran into them head on, killing the whole family. It was sad; the whole town came out for their funeral, even though they didn't treat them very well, when they were alive.

The drunk driver, John James, the town drunk, lived, never to drink again and became the cemetery keeper, planting flowers on each of the five graves, every spring.

As I walked in side of the office, I wiped a tear, I always felt sad over my best friend leaving this world and me so soon, she was only ten.

Mr. Brown had painted and fixed up the old home, making it look very business like and homely, at the same time. There was a front desk, but the chair was empty, I knew he expected me, for I called before I left the house. Just then a very handsome, older man entered the room from his office.

"Ah, you must be the beautiful Cara-Ann." He said with a charming smile that set my heart to racing.

"You've heard of me?" I asked.

"Yes, I heard your parents talk of you, please come into my office, I have everything you asked for, but I must tell you, Cara-Ann by the time your parents hired me, it was too late."

"Then why charge them so much, if you couldn't do anything?" I snapped angrily.

"Your parents made me go to court and that took a lot of my time, I tried to tell them, but you know how suborn they are. Really Car-Ann the city and county had every right to your parents land, they knew for years that the highway would come across there property.

Didn't they tell you that? No, well it's true, they know for years it was coming, they should have taken the offer, and it was fair."

"Fair, in whose eyes? Yours? The city? The county? Not in my eyes or my parents, was any of this fair!" I screamed.

" My parents worked there whole life on that farm, to have you come and take it away for pennies on the dollar and that's fair. Tell me Mr. Brown, if it were your parents, would it still be fair?"

"Please call me Michael, and yes I would have advised my parents the same. Look I know you don't believe me and I understand. Here's all the paper work of your parents case, I made copies, so you can keep them, please read it first, then if you still have questions, you can call me, here's my card." As he talked he pushed a folder full of papers across the desk, holding his hand there until he finished, smiling as he withdrew it.

"Thank you and I will call, I'm sure there will be questions, Mr. Brown." I picked up the folder turned on my heals and left without another word. The frown that replaced his smile when I call him Mr. Brown, said it all. This girl didn't buy his boat load of charm.

One more stop at the city hall, just to show my face. I didn't know what good I could do, until I read the case papers, but it couldn't hurt to ask, and see if I could stir up anyone.

As I turned in, I noticed that Jason was still sitting in the place watching me. He was really starting to creep me out, I though to my self. I parked my car and entered the building with looking at Jason, like I didn't see him. Let's see how he likes that?

City hall was an old building, but had been painted and improved lately. It had a smell of fresh pain and cleanness. At a small desk of to the side sat a young lady answering the phone, I stopped to watch her as she wrote down the message from the caller, I knew her, I couldn't place her, but I knew her.

"May I help you?" she asked as she turned, but when she saw me, her smile changed, she knew me too.

"Cara-Ann the mayor is waiting to talk to you, just go thru that door and to your left, he knows your coming." She said very business like, not giving it away that she knew me but she said my name, before I told her who I was, so in fact she did give it away.

"And you are?" I asked

"Me, Tammy Smith, we went to school together, remember, you better hurry, the mayor doesn't like to wait."

She spat out before answering the phone and pointing again.

I wanted to ask how she and the mayor knew I was coming, but I knew that answer, Jason. Had to be him or the lawyer Mr. Brown.

I walked into office of the mayor, a huge office with an even bigger desk, but then Kris Harper, the mayor was a big man too. He stood six feet five without his boots on and when he walked up to you, he seemed to take all the space up, leaving you with no choice but to see him.

"My, my, my what a peasant surprise to see you Cara-Ann." He had gotten up and walked over to me when I came in; he now hugged me in a bare hug, that over powered me with his after shave. I pushed off making him laugh.

"Now Cara-Ann, don't be like that, I watched you grow up child, your daddy and I were best friends once…"

"Yea once, not now Kris, not now. Tell me what

happened and I'll go.

Kris then told the same story that the lawyer had said, blaming my folks, saying they knew about it for years and ending with, we need the highway.

"I'm sorry about your dad, how's he doing anyhow?" At last he asked when he was finished, trying to act caring, when I knew he had not been to see my dad, and didn't care about his health, except maybe his death.

"Great, may live ten more years, doctors think." I said, knowing it was a lie, but not wanting this man to know the truth.

"Good, good, tell him I asked for him. Anything else I can help you with? Got some business I need to take care of" And with that he began to escort me out.

"You stop in and see me anytime, ok." He said as he shut the door, not waiting for an answer from me, pushing me out.

Had I said something to upsets him, perhaps about my dad's heath.

I walked out waving bye at Tammy, never did like that girl, I mumbled to myself, looking down, I walked right into Jason.

"What girl?" He asked looking back at the city hall.

"Tammy, she's a sweetheart." He said as he stood in my

way.

"Ah yes, I remembered, you two dated after we broke up.
Remembering the stories I had heard after leaving for college.

"Come on Cara honey, it was one date and it was just to hurt you, you're the one I loved then and still do honey, don't look so surprised, I've been waiting for your return, I knew you would come back to me one day."

"No Jason, No. I didn't come back for you and I don't care how you feel. Now move I have to go, I don't have time for this."

I pushed past him reaching for the truck door, when I noticed it was a jar. I knew I had closed it, good thing I took all my paperwork into the city hall with me.

I jumped in started up the truck and backed up, leaving Jason standing there with a smile on his face.

He had moved past creepy to scaring the hell out of me. I turned the old truck toward home; I was shaking so much I had to grab the steering wheel had to hold on to it.

I started thinking about Jason, he had always been controlling, it was on of the reason, I jumped ship.

He had to know all my friend's and what I was doing all the time, at first it was kind of cool, thinking he loved me that much but later on, not so cool.

He would get angry at me if I didn't tell him where I was going or where I had been and who I was going with.

He would call first thing in the morning and last thing at night before bed. My parents didn't care for the way he kept so tight of reigns on me. They had begged me to get away from Jason.

It was hard for me to do, but it was the best thing I had done for myself. My mother said he called for weeks asking about me, asking where I was? They told him nothing; the three of them didn't like each other, that's why I found it strange that mother would tell of my coming home, I must remember to ask about that.

I kept a close eye on the rear view mirror as I drove back home, thank goodness I saw no other cars, front or back. It was a nice day to drive and think.

I didn't trust Jason or his new friends at city hall, and it would not surprise me if they got a little rough in getting what they wanted, and if they wanted the farm, they would pull out all the stops to get it. I couldn't wait to talk to my friend, the lawyer, I had stopped and made copies at the post office, mailing a copy over night to her, she would read them and let me know if any thing was wrong,

Mary had been my friend sense I moved to the city, her I trusted. I would read them tonight and see if I could find anything.

Something was wrong with the whole thing I knew it; I had to find it and save the farm for my mother and dad.

The horses and cows had been sold, and the fields unplanted, they too sold.

It didn't look like the home I grew up on, so empty and bare.

Sadly I looked away from the land and to the house in the distance. It too was so badly in shape, it made me cry.

I had loved growing up here and would have stayed, except for no college and Jason. I wondered if I would think about staying now.

If I saved the farm. I had my degree and could work from home on the computer and internet, one nice thing about updating the town, cable and internet.

We had phones growing up, but anyone not in our town, was long distance, change is good, sometimes.

I pulled up to the barn, backing in the truck and parking it. There were holes in the walls from old age, it was sad to see daddy's pride in such bad shape.

As with any farmer he kept his barn and tools in great working shape. Daddy loved the land just as his daddy before and his daddy before him. A long list of farmers and ranchers, till an only child at home turned out to be a girly girl. Me. I had tired to love it, I took FFA classes in school, but it didn't help.

I wanted to be an artist, live in the city, go to play's, dress up to the nine. So I did just that. Now I felt a little guilty for leaving, but glad I went, all the same.

Chapter 03
"The Homecoming"
By Deana Rae Higgins

Losing daddy

Mother was sitting at the kitchen table when I came in the back door. She looked tired and sad; daddy being sick was taking its toll on her.

Her hair had turned gray and her eyes had bags under them. Even her shoulders sagged.

I kissed her cheek and sat to talk. I told her of my day and about seeing Jason.

"I knew it!" She shouted, getting excited.

We talked, while we cooked dinner. We talked while eating, about all the time we missed, while I was away. We talked and laughed, until it was time for her to go upstairs' to dad.

I then settled in for some reading, and even thou I was not a lawyer; I could tell that there were things out of order.

I fell asleep, thinking about the land, and my parents. I dreamed of Jason. I dreamed I had stayed, and in my dream, I wasn't as strong, as I was now. Jason had taken control of my life and I had no say in anything. In my dream, I was weak and followed Jason like a puppy. I dreamed of his helping the fat city hall boys with there land grab.

I saw money change hands, from theirs to his. I saw my parents kicked out into the streets, penniless. I was numb with pain, yet I showed no emotion.

I awoke scared and shaking. I was wet from sweat and crying. I now knew that it was better I had left here when I did, and that the me now, was going to fight for what was right.

I couldn't go back to sleep, so I rose and took a long bath. I put in the bath salts; mother had bought for me, and soaked all my fears away.

I had just finished dressing, when I heard mother screaming. I ran in to my parent's room, as mother ran out.

"Stay with him, I must call 911" She screamed as she ran downstairs.

Father was lying on the bed, head to the side, and white as a ghost. He looked dead. I couldn't see any movement, or any signs of breathing. I stood there in fear, scared to go closer wishing I could leave. I didn't know what to do.

My father had been such a strong man, and so very smart. Tall and proud of who he was. This was nothing like the man who raised me. Who taught me how to ride a bike, how to do math, and play spades for fun.

He taught me to ride a horse and rope a cow. How to plow the fields and plant a garden.

This body was a shadow of the man I loved and yet it was him.

The ambulance came quick; father was put on life support and taken to the hospital. County again. I heard the words, heart giving out.

My head began to hurt. Mother had gone in the ambulance with father; I was to bring the truck I was shaking so hard it was hard for me to drive.

Part of me did not wish to go, yet I had to, as an adult.

What would I find? I couldn't help wondering if perhaps daddy would be better off dead, but then I felt bad for thinking such a thing. Poor mother, how would she hold up?

My parents had been married for so long, both of them very young when they married. All mother knew was being a wife to my father. If I lost my dad would I lose my mother too? The though scared me.

I saw mother right away, curled up in a waiting room chair, her feet tucked under her.

She looked like a lost child, my heart sank, and it must be bad. I sat beside her, taking her in my arms.

She laid her head on my shoulder and began to cry light, soft sobs as I held her, and rocked us both back and forth.

No words were spoke, there was none needed.

We sat that way for the longest, and then slowly we got

up to stretch, untangling from each others arms.

I went to get some hot tea for us. When I returned, we sat in silence as we each drank our tea.

After about two hours, the doctor came to see us, I watched as mother heard the news, coma, no brain waves and loss of oxygen.

I watched her face turn white, with tears streaming down her cheek. I stepped up to hold her, I though, she would break.

Instead she straightened up her back and spoke very softly.

"I'll call my son and then we'll decide as a family what to do, thank you doctor for being so honest. You have my number; please call if there is any change." She then turned without another word and walked out.

We rode home in silence, both of us lost in our thoughts, neither able to grasp that father was gone.

When we arrived home, I sat about making us tea and sandwiches; mother sat at the phone table and made the hardest phone call she ever had to make. To my brother.

When she finished we sat in silence to eat. When mother was done she rose, speaking softly she said.

"I need a nap." and went upstairs to cry.

I knew if she needed me, she would call for me. I cleaned up the kitchen then sat down to cry myself, as the numbness wore off and realty set in.

My father was gone, only his body hung on. I was so

grateful that James would be here soon. James was a big time architect. He will put the scare into those men down town, I though laughing. James had wanted to stay on the farm but daddy would not hear of it. James had been top of his class and gotten a free ride thru collage. He was ten years older then me, and father wasn't worried about the farm and who would run it, until later on.

I always suspect that my father had wanted another boy, but got me instead.

I had always though father wanted me to stay home because he though I wasn't as smart as James.

Growing up all I heard about was how smart my brother was. I hated living in his shadow. Even in school, I was compared to James, the teachers always made remarks about how smart he was and why wasn't I like him.

As I walked upstairs I passed James' room, the door shut. I opened it and looked in, to see if the bed needed making, but I should have known better, everything was clean and the bed freshly made.

Mother had made up both our rooms; she knew it was going to be needed soon.

James' room was so different then mine. Mine was more like a princess' room and his like a shrine to the best son in the whole world.

There were pictures of him in his glory, in high school. Head of this, head of that, leader of everything. There were awards and letters of recommendations on every wall. His hat and gown from graduation hung up, in a glass case over his bed, made by daddy too.

Every where there was proof of my parents love. I felt like I was standing in a museum of some sorts. I left, shutting the door. I entered my room, shut the door, fell on to my bed and cried my self to sleep.

Again I dreamed of Jason, of past times we shared, our friends, our school outings. Jason had been my first love. I had such high hopes for us, back then in high school.

In my dream Jason and I were standing, alone, talking, when suddenly he grabbed me by the neck and started choking me, I fought with all my might, scratching his face, but that only made him madder.

I could see the light in his eyes as he enjoyed strangling me. I could hear his laughter as I started to fade out.

I awoke with a start grasping for air, scared out of my wits, certain that my dreams were telling me to be careful of Jason.

Next morning mother and I were sitting at the table, breakfast over, but in no hurry to rush to clean up, when in walked my brother James.

He had taken the red eye and rented a car. He looked tired but well. James was rather tall, like dad, six-three. He had mothers blue eyes and brown hair like mine and dads. He was a very handsome man, and in great shape, I noticed.

He walked in and fell to his knees at mother's feet and grabbing her, holding her as he cried, making her and me cry too. I joined in on the hugging and crying, the three of us crying over the best man we all had known.

When at last we had no more tears to cry, we made tea and talked, to catch up on all the news, avoiding the one subject we didn't want to discuss. Daddy and what should be done.

We laughed at good times we had had, and the funny things the kids had done. James showed us pictures of both his daughter and son, twins, age five. Mother and I both in aw over how beautiful they both were.

We looked at pictures of his wife, Kelly, so slim and trim, a great beauty herself. They felt it best not to bring the twins to a funeral.

So we started talking about what to do, about daddy. We would pull the plug and give his peace at last. No way would he had wanted to live this way, all three of us agreed.

We talked of his funeral and what daddy wanted. The small burial plots that he and mother had bought many years ago, at Westlake cemetery. Father and mother both wanted a small service.

Father would get daisies, his favorite flower.

We left in James rented car to go to the hospital, there was no reason to wait.

At the hospital we stood by fathers bed, praying and crying together.

Daddy was attached to machines that did everything for him, he looked white as the sheet surrounding him.

We watched as they turned off the machine breathing for him, taking his breath away. We watched as the life drained from his sick body.

We watched as his body died, knowing that daddy was gone already. We cried and held each other as the red line went flat.

The doctor called his death at 6:45 p.m. and we cried more tears. Then slowly both my brother and myself, each kissed daddy's cold cheek, leaving the room and mother, giving her time alone to say goodbye to her husband of thirty-five years.

When she came out we drove home in silence. Daddy was gone forever to us all.

When we arrived home, mother again left for her room to rest, James and I sat to talk over dinner and tea.

While James heated up some of mom's home made cream of chicken soup I ran upstairs and got the papers the lawyer had given me.

I watched as he read each page, his face showing his anger the more he read. I remembered my friend and gave her a call to see what she had to say, putting her on speaker phone so James could hear what she said too.

"I'm coming to help, this is the sorriest court papers that I've ever seen, everything about it screams fraud. I'm so sorry about your dad, give my best to your mom. I'll see you soon. Guys please be care…" And the phone went dead.

Something was wrong, I had known it, so had James when he read the papers.

The phone didn't come back on and the next day, as we

drove to town, we saw the wires had been cut. They weren't even hiding it. They wanted our farm and would stop at nothing to get it, would that included murder I wondered.

We drove over to the next town to set up dad's funeral.

My parents had gotten a package deal when they bough their burial plots. It included everything they needed to bury my father.

We picked out a light blue lining for the casket, my dad's favorite color, we ordered several dozen daisies to lay on top of his casket and grave, and we ordered his headstone. I read it out loud, it sounded good.

"James Raye Sr. 1952-2007, beloved father, grandfather and husband." A simple headstone for a simple man.

After we had decided everything that was needed, and signed all the papers, we left and went out to dinner on James.

Dinner was great but none of us really noticed, each of us lost in our own toughs.

We tired to fell the empty gaps of conversation but gave up after awhile and eat in silence.

As we drove home we saw the phone company fixing the cut phone line.

"Sometimes it pays to be on a party line." Mother stated, making us laugh.

We all knew how much daddy hated the party line, main reason he had gotten the cell phone for himself.

He hated that every time he picked up the phone there was someone on there gossiping. Mother loved it and would pick up the phone and join in on the talk, talking about all there neighbor's. She would spend long periods of her day talking on the phone.

Mother had gotten rid of daddy's cell phone when he got sick, a waste of money, she said.

Mother and I went up stairs on arrival, leaving James downstairs to call his wife. We hugged then went to our separate bedrooms, to each cry ourselves to sleep. I awoke early in the morning, again from bad dreams about Jason, only this time I slid in bed with my mother, sleeping like a baby.

Mothers bed protecting me from bad dreams.

Chapter 04
"The Homecoming"
By Deana Rae Higgins

A family once more

The next morning I slept in, being in mothers bed made me feel so safe, and I was so tired.

I awoke fresh and feeling great until I remembered about daddy's death.

I hurried to dress and go downstairs, and find mother and James. I found mother sitting alone at the table talking on the phone.
When she saw me, she said goodbye and hung up.

"Mother you could have talked your friends." I said as I sat down.

"No it's alright, I was done anyhow. Did you sleep well in my bed child?" She asked, touching my hand, as her eyes laughed.

"Yes mama, it was the best sleep in so long. Where's James?" I asked as I looked around.

"Outside, doing some work around here, I told him not to worry, but he wouldn't listen to me, said he needed to stay busy, but really I'm glad, there was some things that needed fixed.

I could have paid Jack, the young man who picked you up at the train station, did you notice the changes they made at the station, nice huh.

James has always has hated waiting, just like your father, and he was getting under foot in my kitchen, I can't believe that your dad has…" Her voice caching as she finished thinking about daddy.

Just then, we heard voices outside, we both turned to look at the door just as Jack, the handyman, who had picked me up at the air port, came in.

"Betty, I'm so sorry about James. I wish I had been here to help you. Do you need me to do anything? Has all the arrangements been made? I could help you. You sure?" Jack asked seeing her shake her head no when he asked to help.

I couldn't believe he used my parent's first names, he wasn't much older then me, I thought.

Mother seemed to like this young man, so maybe he wasn't as bad as I was thinking. I still didn't trust him.

“Jack, you remember my daughter, and this handsome gentleman behind you is my son, James Jr., now please sit and have tea with us.” Mother stated as she pulled out a chair.

“I can’t Betty, I must get back to work, and I just came by to see if I could do anything for you, but I see you’re in good hands, let me know if I can do anything for you.”

And with a nod to James he turned and left, without a word or nod to me.

“Such a sweet guy, his mother died when he was young, and his father ran off with a rodeo. Been on his own, his whole life.” Mother seemed to be Jacks favorite fan.

“If you say so Mother, I don’t think he’s a very nice man, rude if you ask me, and you don’t know he could be in on all that’s happened.” I said with a frown.

Mother just laughed, knowing I really found him attractive and went back to fixing breakfast for us, she whistled as she cooked, happy to be cooking for her babies, even grown up babies.

We spent the day talking, and cleaning for the service, there be people here and neither mother nor I wanted them to see a dusty home.

James used his time working outside in the yard.

The funeral had been planed for Wednesday at the old church in town; daddy would go only for weddings and funerals, it seemed right.

Today was Monday and there was a lot to do, cleaning and cooking. We made pies and cakes.

James had gone shopping while mother and I slept, he had bough stuff for the dinner, a roast, ham and all the fixings, he knew mother couldn't afford it.

It was fun to spend the day with mother in the kitchen, watching her and helping her, but all the while talking, like we haven't done in ages.

I missed mother so much when I was away, she was my best friend as well as the greatest mom.

When as last the day was near end, the three of us sat and ate sandwiches and hot homemade soup, drinking hot tea with honey.

It was the best time we had had, just the three of us, but the time there was sadness, we missed daddy so.

We talked about all the wonderful things daddy had done for each one of us. Like building mothers stairs when she had a huge staircase on the other side of the house that ran upstairs to the library and a spare bedroom, that mother used as a sewing room.

When I left home they closed off the right side, it was too big for just the two of them, and there was a great room and study downstairs as well as the rooms upstairs.

We cleaned them and took all the covers off the

furniture, and even brought some chairs and tables from upstairs to fill in. It was so beautiful, it made both me and mother cry when as last we had finished.

James when he came in, stopped in aw, it had been closed up for so long, it looked like it did in our youth, dad would be proud.

Mother had a huge dining table in the sitting room, and that's where we choice to eat our dinner that night and talk about dad. A perfect time in a perfect place. Mother and children in a circle of love.

When we had laughed and cried over and over, we rose, I shooed away mother and James to bed while I cleaned up, they looked so tired.

"Goodnight Cara-Ann, I didn't might you sleeping in my bed last night, so maybe if you want, you could come up when you finish, goodnight son, I'm so glad you're here to help me, I love both of you, and now I'm going to take a long bath, I suggest you dirty children do the same."

We laughed as she left to go upstairs. James followed her up with a quick kiss and a goodnight sis, missed you."

I cleaned up the kitchen, called and left messages for friends, talked to Mary, my lawyer friend, who was coming up for the funeral, I couldn't wait to hear what she had to say, she had been writing letters to the state on our behalf about our land, so it would be really nice to see her. I had no boyfriend, as I hadn't dated much after leaving here and Jason.

At the though of Jason a sliver ran down my spine giving me the chills, bath time, I ran for the stairs, cold now and scared to be alone downstairs.

I soaked in a nice hot tub with my bath salts, then hurried down the hall to mothers room, she was already in bed, sleeping, I slid in and passed out, sleeping with no dreams at all. A great night sleep for us all, I hoped.

When I awoke mother was again downstairs, this time talking to James, they both looked up and smiled when I entered the room.

We had always been close as a family but now the three of us pulled together to bond tight as a family.

Mother and I decided to clean up daddy's clothes and stuff that James didn't want and pack it up for the charity box at church, all day long as we went thru dad's stuff. Stopping only for lunch.

Mother and I found several treasure's, dad's watch, pictures of his parents and letters he had wrote to mother before he got sick, unopened letters, she put these aside to read later when she was alone.

We found his old will leaving the farm to mother and then on her death to James and myself.

We found small gifts that we had giving him for his birthdays and Christmas, new wallet, new watch, new shirts and ties, all new in the box and unused.

Mother and I picked out a new tie for dad to wear with his blue suit we had sent over to the funeral home. We would send James to drop it off, latter today.

Then went we thought we had found it all, we found a map with a red x on it, it looked old and very special, something we best look at with James.

We packed up everything and set it by mom's bedroom door; we would have James drop it off on his way to the funeral home.

Then we rearranged mothers stuff to fill the empty space left by the removal of dad's stuff, we put on clean sheets and hung some of her sewing, wall hangings she had made on the walls.

The room looked so different and very modern. A nice change for mother.

We had forgot all about, losing the farm, mother had put all of us ahead of her self so long, she was having fun, fixing her room for herself, we all knew she would miss dad so much I wanted to make it easier for her, and then I knew my answer. I would stay, to be with my mother, all else didn't matter in the long term of things.

You only have one mother and one father unless you're lucky, and I had missed so much with my father, I didn't get to tell him I loved him, or goodbye, I would not miss out with my mother.

After we loaded up James rental car and sent him to the next town, with dad's stuff to drop off, dad's tie, to go to the funeral home and a list of stuff we needed from the store, we sat and had dinner alone, just mom and I, we knew James would eat junk food in town.

We didn't speak much during dinner, too tired from working and too sad to think. Tomorrow was a day we did not look for ward to.

It would take all our energy and strength to face it, but thank goodness we had each other. I sent mother ahead while I cleaned the kitchen, giving her time alone before I crashed in her room again.

I was standing at the sink when I heard a noise, I turned to look outside and there stood Jason, watching me. I screamed dropping the plate I was holding and backed up. Mother came running in.

"What's wrong?" She screamed as she ran in, breathing hard, wearing only her housecoat.

All I could do was point at the window, mother turned looked outside and cussed under her breath, shocking me.

"Damn it Jason, get your ass in here, now boy!" she yelled out the window.

I then moved over to the window to stand besides my mother, should have know she would scare as easy as me, not mother; she was the bravest person I knew.

"Sorry Cara-Ann, Ms Raye, sorry. Didn't mean to scare, just heard about James and wanted to come by and see if you needed anything. Real sorry Cara, really, its just you looked so pretty, there standing at the sink, washing dishes, sorry about the dish. Want me to sweep it up?" He asked as he pointed to the dish I had dropped.

He had just walked in without knocking, why I hadn't locked the door after James left and stayed up to wait to let him in. I would now.

Mother laughing turned to leave, aware of her nudeness under her house coat.

"Next time come during the day and don't sneak around here Jason, and Cara-Ann lock that door, I gave James a key." She shouted back as she ascended up the stairs.

I turned and faced Jason all fear gone replaces with anger.

"What is your problem, don't you get it? I don't want you around me, you do not need to worry about me, and I'm not your girlfriend anymore!" I shouted at him.

"Aw honey…come here." Opening his arms as he walked toward me.

"NO!" I screamed as he did.

"Cara-Ann, you ok?" Mother asked from the top of the stairs.

"Yes mother I'm fine, I be there in a second." I yelled back.

Then it happened, my dream.

He was on me in a second putting his hand over my mouth to silence me, my heart started beating so fast, I couldn't catch my breath, he then moved his hands around my neck letting me catch small breaths, he held me there against the fridge, his face in mine, smiling this sick smile.

He scared the hell out of me, I tired to break free but he just laughed and held tighter, until I couldn't breathe again.

"Don't forget honey, your mine all mine. I own you! And you and me got a date to get to know each other all over again."

As he talked he started running his hands over my body. I tired to push him away but he grabbed my neck harder, so I stopped, grasping for air, I could not move.

He pushed his feet inside of my feet, pushing my legs apart, running his hand up my leg slowly holding me with his right.

"I hate you!" I spat at him, spitting in his face.

Tightening his grip with his right hand he shut off my air, he then slapped me across the face with his left, stunning me.

Then pushing himself against me, he started rubbing his man hood against me, laughing as he did so.

I couldn't breath and felt as if I might die when he let go of me making me so off balance, I fell to the floor in a crumpled ball against the fridge. Jason then turned and walked out.

“Don’t forget baby, we got a date, like it or not, don’t matter to me, either way, I’m taking back what’s mine.” He spat out as he left, locking and shutting the door behind him.

I rose, still trying to catch my breath, I checked the door, even thought I saw him lock it, my lungs seemed to have shrunk, when at last I filled my lungs with air, tears started streaming down my face.

I was still sitting there crying when James came home. Thinking I was crying over dad, he held me as I cried and I let him, till all my tears were gone.

“Better?” he asked as I pulled away.

“Yes, thank you, I love you.” Was all I could say as I kissed his cheek and ran upstairs.

I ran to my room ran a hot bath and cried more tears until I was so exhausted I dressed in my pajama’s and slipped in bed with mother.

Tomorrow I would think about it, tomorrow was the last though as I fell asleep. Only this time I had bad dreams that made me toss and turn all night.

Dreams of Jason and my own death.

Chapter 05
"The Homecoming"
By Deana Rae Higgins

Daddy's funeral

The day started at dawn, it found the three of us downstairs drinking very strong coffee.

None of us felt like eating breakfast, the day we dreaded have come at last, daddy's funeral.

We didn't talk, each of us lost in our own thoughts. It was pouring rain, and had been sense midnight. It was if the world was crying with us.

Somehow it made us feel better; it would have been hard to feel sadness on a wonderful bright sunny day.

Rainy days would never be the same for any of us. At eight we rose and each went to dress, the funeral was at ten this morning.

I had to borrow a black skirt and top from mother, black had always been her favorite color, I wondered how she would feel about it now that she had to wear it, in morning for dad.

We met in the hall when we finished dressing, me in moms outfit, which fit pretty good, mother in her best black dress, that was dad's favorite and James in his best black suit, we held hands and said a request for the day, that all would go right.

We rode in James rental car, a nice new sedan with leather seats, a dark blue, perfect for the ride in the funeral recession. Dad would be proud.

It stopped raining as we walked out on the porch, like someone turned off the water works; we looked at each other and had to laugh.

"Just like your father to control the weather on the day he's buried." Mother stated making us laugh again.

I'm sure anyone who saw us would think we had gone crazy from grief or didn't care about daddy's death, but the opposite was true, we knew daddy didn't want to live the way he was living life at the end, so for that fact we were glad, that at last daddy's was at peace. That and we had cried so much we had no sadness left.

I had told no one about what had happened last night with Jason; I didn't want to worry my family and today belong to daddy. I wore a scarf to cover the bruises on my neck.

We were the first to arrive, so while mother made sure daddy's tie was straight and said her goodbyes alone, James and I made sure that no one entered until she was done, we gave her five minutes then we had to let people in, they had shown up in droves.

It brought tears to my eyes to see how much daddy was loved by his friends and neighbors; he had grown up here and lived here all his life.

James and I took our seats by mother and watched as every seat filled. The overflow stood every where there was a spot, the small church had never seen so many at one time. There were flowers of every kind, every where you looked by daddy was some huge flower arrangement.

Our simple daisies had been pushed to the back, barely seen.

Mother wasn't very happy about the show the town had made, it made her mad that the same people never came to see him, when he was alive, nor did they turn out when daddy's barn burned two years ago, and daddy had to rebuild part of it the best he could alone.

James and I had a different felling about all the hoop la. It made us proud to see.

Our father was a very proud and honest man, dad always did the right thing and was always willing to help those who needed help, he was always taking mom's canned goods to some family in the winter who needed food.

I remember times we scraped up money for food only to have dad scare it with the family of twelve kids down the street, we would cook it and help dad with it, because you either went along with daddy or you got left at home with nothing, and he would take the whole dinner to there home and we would sit at there table like guests, laughing at there jokes, sharing our dinner.

The family's we met and had dinner with that way was too many to number.

As we sat there each watching, lost in our own thoughts, certain people begin to stand out to us and we would point them out to each other.

The man at the bank, the farm workers, the salesmen's and of course the town hall biggies.

The Mayor and his buddies had front roll seats.

I looked for Jason, trying to hold myself in check, but when at last I saw him, he smiled a wicket smile that froze my blood and made me start to shake, I turned, trying to catch myself but my mother had seen me and wanted to know what was wrong, she looked to see whom it was I saw, and when she saw it was Jason, she whispered in my ear, we will talk later about him.

It helped knowing I wouldn't have to be along in my private hell. Mother and I would sit down latter and together decide how best to handle Jason. Mother would not feel the fear I do and would know what to do.

The service was very nice, the choir sang hymn's that reminded me of day's long ago, when I was young and came to Sunday school and how much I missed it. I didn't know the new preacher, nor did he know daddy but he did know mother and I made a mental note to ask her later how. He did a great job, and I like him, right away, even thou he looked too young to be a preacher.

There were many people who stood to tell stories, men who worked with daddy, women who's dinner table we shared and children who remembered his generosity.

The three of us sat in total aw, some of the stories we had never heard, and the rest we had known the impact of daddy's life until we heard it out loud. It was amazing to hear such greats things said about our dad and husband.

When at last just about everyone in the church had spoken about daddy, James Raye Sr. more then half the crowd had tears.

We closed his casket, taking our last look at the man we loved and watched as he was carried by so many to the gravesite behind the church, we all walked behind carrying flowers for his grave.

All of us stood three quarters around his casket and grave plot, ten rolls deep, holding hands and praying, it was a very tender moment for all of us.

I had closed my eyes and then taken a hand hold of the person standing next to me, when I opened my eyes I saw that it was Jason, I pulled away and moved away, putting my brother beside Jason, both laugh and began to talk like old friends angering me more.

I tried so hard to handle what was going on inside me but I was really having a hard time of it.

When at last we turned to leave, James and I stood back, waiting for mother, who needed a minute more to say bye, everyone else left leaving us alone.

I looked under the tree in the middle of the cemetery, to Jane my childhood friends grave, I saw new flowers on it.

Her grave was in tip top form, somehow it saddened me and thrilled me at the same time, she deserved the best but shouldn't be here, She should be standing next to be, still my best friend.

When mother had said her goodbye for the last time, we left to go home, we had tons of hungry folks coming over who expected to taste some of mom's great cooking. I was so happy we had cleaned and that James had fixed some things, I hadn't found my friend Mary, the lawyer, I hoped nothing had happened, she should have been here by now.

There where cars everywhere when we pulled up to our home, woman with dishes of great smelling food stood every where, we could feed an army I though, but then guess we were I laughed. Feeding our friends and enemies alike.

We opened the doors and they filled in filling our small home wall to wall. Mother and I sat about laying out all the food with the help of our neighbors while James jetted around the room meeting everyone, like a prized bull or prized bull's son. I don't think I've had ever seen James so proud of his dad. It was really nice to see, I just hope dad knew it.

Jason hadn't come to the house, I thanked god. I was

able to relax and enjoy seeing old friends, in fact as I sorted thru the people I noticed that a lot of the city hall workers hadn't come to the house, back stabbers. Such phony people I though..

Mother seemed to be holding up, very well, but she looked tired. She was enjoying seeing all her friends together, I noticed.

The day seemed to drag on forever, there was food of every kind and desserts to make your mouth water. People ate, drank and visited for hours.
Everywhere I turned there was a hug for me from everyone. Most of the kids from school that James and I had grown up with, moved out of town after gradation, but there was some who stayed, and it was so nice to visit with them and see pictures of kids and spouses. It was better sweet visit, all around.

At dusk, they began to leave, clearing out the house. A lot of mothers friends stayed to help clean up, and I was ever so grateful, I didn't have to do it all.

James saw the men out the door, shaking hands with all of daddy's old friends,

I followed mother and her friends around hanging on every word, they seemed to have a bond, that I'm not sure I have with anyone, and it trilled me to watch them.

They acted more like sisters, the five of them, I though, it was nice and I wanted it.

There was Janet, the Mayor's wife, Marcy, the druggist's wife, Midge, her nurse friend and Sally, her best friend, forever, it seemed, I could see why my parents chose to stay in a small town and raise there family here.

It had a closeness about that seemed unreal yet very family like. My mother had spent a lot of time with her friends, thru the years.

They would have quilting bee's, cooking parties, canning fest's, birthday parties, any time, any place lunch's.

I saw them pull mother aside and whisper something to her, that made her smile ear to ear, I couldn't hear it, but it must have been great news.

Mothers mood changed and she seemed much more at peace, and then it happened, our whole world changed in a spilt second.

Mother collapsed. One second she was standing, laughing and the next she went down. She was out cold.

We called the ambulance and took her to the hospital in town, James went in the ambulance with her to put the whole thing on his credit card, I stayed to finish up and lock the doors, it took two seconds to rush everyone out and close up the kitchen.

I turned to leave, but in my way, there he stood. Jason.

I never made it to the hospital for mother, instead I was taken for my self to save my life, Jason had not come to pay a social call, he came to repay me for all the hurt he felt when I left town.

He came to make me his again, his lover, his woman and his property. He came to put me in line, he said as he hit me full force in the jaw, knocking me out cold.

Chapter 06
"The Homecoming"
By Deana Rae Higgins

Jason's revenge

I awoke with a headache and my jaw hurt something awful, I couldn't move my arms, as they were tied together above my head, to mother's headboard, I saw, when I moved my head to see my hands. I was alone, I didn't understand what was going on, I remembered Jason hitting me.

But where was he now? I turned as far as I could to look around mother's room, and then I heard him enter the room.

"Your awake, was thinking I would have to keep this pleasure all to myself and I just didn't want to rob you of our reunion, I wish I could trust you not to run but I know in time you'll remember our love, so we'll pretend that it's a game we're playing, and this time its all my time to show you what you been missing baby, no, no don't cry now, you know you like it like this baby, don't fight me baby, I don't want to hurt you, your my girl."

As he talked he moved to the bed sitting beside me, at fist thinking I could get him to untie my hands, I tried to play along with his game, but when it became apparent that it wasn't going to happen, I tried kick him hard.

He jumped on top of me holding my legs down so I couldn't move, he leaned in to kiss me and again I spit in his face, mad now.

At first he laughed then slapped me hard across my face, I could taste blood.

"Want to play baby, you know I really think that's what you need is a good beating to put you in place, like a dog, you need to know just who is master here, understand baby, me, me, got that." He grabbed my leaning in for another kiss, this time I met him coming in, like I wanted to kiss him back and I bit down hard on his lip and held on, I felt my teeth go all the way thru his lip and this time I tasted his blood.

He head butted me, and I let go, I felt so dazed I had to close my eyes to steady myself, my head hurt so bad I couldn't think and every time I tried to move I wanted to throw up, when at last I opened my eyes, I could hardly see, there was blood running down my face in a steady stream across my eyes.

I could hear Jason laughing loud, and the room seemed to be moving with every laugh he made. I felt my clothes ripped from body, like I was a rag doll, and then I was nude. I tried to move, sense Jason had gotten off my legs to take my clothes off but I couldn't, my legs didn't seem to hear me, yell move.

"Please." I started to beg but Jason put his hand over my mouth to shut me up, and with on quick movement he was on top again, this time he had spread my legs wide and climbed on top of me, entering me with a hard force that ripped me open to him.

He started kissing me and I tried to stop him and again he hit me full force in the face with his fist, chipping my front tooth.

"Hell with it bitch, kiss this." Shoving himself in my face, and then down my throat, hard, jamming himself completely into my mouth until I couldn't breathe.

With each movement I made trying to free myself so I could breathe he took it as my enjoying it.

"Yes, he screamed, I knew you missed me, that's it baby, oh yes, you do love it. Don't you baby?"

My lungs felt like fire had replaced the air in them.

The room began to fade in and out, the light above the bed growing dimmer and dimmer, my whole body begged for air, the pain I felt slowing fading away too.

Just then he pulled away and the air came rushing in making my lungs gasp for more and then he shoved himself hard into my open mouth again, closing off my air supply, controlling my life and my death until he wanted me to die and I knew, in my heart he would kill me.

Not for one second, did I think he would leave me alive, how could he, I would tell, he knew that.

He saw the affect he was having on me and he like it, a lot.

His eyes turned black as he began to understand that he controlled my every second of my time on earth.

My life was in his hands and he was loving every second of it, he would pull himself out and then grab my face and mouth and jam himself as far as he could, watching my face the whole time, enjoying it, pulling out as my color changed from white to purple then back to white when he pulled himself out.

He did this over and over, until I begged him to kill me.

"Oh baby I love you, your so soft, so sweet and tight baby, just how I like my baby, I'm so glad you saved your self for me, I was worried you go to that big city of yours and fuck everybody, you met, but not my girl, nope I told them all, not my girl, I wish you would understand you are mine forever, till death us do part and if you don't start acting better, I might have to do something to your mom, like I did that nosy friend of yours from the city. Oh now I have your attention huh."

"Mary." Was all I could gasp between breaths, as he pulled out of my mouth, he then mounted me again, entering me from below, hurting me as he jammed himself deep inside me, holding one of his hands over my mouth, to control my breathing as he raped me.

Then in one quick movement he flipped me over, laying me on my belly, as he still held my mouth from behind, leaving a small space between his fingers for me to gasp for air as he entered my anis, not caring how much he hurt me. In fact hurting me seemed to get him off more then the actual sex.

When I tried to bite his fingers he again slapped me hard from the back across my ears making the ring. I gave up and relaxed, taking all his fun away.

He finished and withdrew himself from inside me and off me; he flipped me over again to face him, grabbing my throat and shutting off my air supply again, looking into my eyes, kissing my face, letting go long enough to let me breathe, but still holding his hand there, as he started to kiss me, forcing his tongue into my mouth, I could taste beer and cigarette's on his breath, I had no more fight to fight him off, he took this as my giving in and started moving his tongue all around the inside of my mouth.

He then stopped and untied my hands; I had lost all feelings in my hands from the tightness of the ruff rope he had used from the barn.

He then kissed both and lay then down beside me on the

bed.

"I'm sorry Cara-Ann, but you'll see it will be ok, you understand now, it will be ok." And then he walked out and I passed out cold.

I was bloody from my head to my knees, and I was slowing bleeding to death, from the damage of his ripping me open when he raped me, I could feel life slowing draining out of me. My head had a large cut and a huge bump from his head butt.

I had no sense of time, I woke up several times, only to pass out again. I couldn't move with out getting dizzy and I was very week from loss of blood, I prayed for help and waited for it to come.

At one point, I felt so bad when I awoke that I knew I was dying, right here in my mother and fathers bed, my poor mother was my last though as I passed out again, the next time I awoke I was in the hospital and I knew I was safe for now, my head hurt so bad, I had to sleep, and feel asleep to heal and dream, and dream I did, I went over and over everything that Jason had did and said, I would not forget anything.

I would remember I had to, he had to pay. What was it he said about Mary? Something about mother too, but every time I woke it faded a little more, like some bad dream when you fall asleep again.

I did a lot of sleeping and dreaming, once in a while, I would wake, sometimes at night when I could see nothing, sometimes during the day and

I could hear life going on around me.

The dreams I had, all good, of day's gone bye.

I dreamed of daddy a lot, calling to me, telling me it was going to be ok. At times when I woke mother was by my side, other times of her friends, but always someone. I was never alone.

At first I would stay awake for seconds, but as time went by slowly I started staying awake more. It was to talk, my jaw was wired shut, Jason had broke it in three places.

There where flowers every where I could look, the smell was so heavenly.

As I began to emerge from my cocoon, the same question was asked, I would turn my head and pretend I had no knowledge of who did this to me. I was afraid and needed time to think without the sedition that they kept injecting in my IV. One day when I awoke mother was there, I wrote that, I couldn't see who, the question was never asked again.

"The cops seem to have nothing to go on, but they have been catching some tips from a pawn shop, who ever it was went thru everything in all the bedrooms, looking for something, he took my jewelry, that your grandmother gave me, wasn't much but enough to pawn, I guess.

Didn't seem to take anything from you or James, Cops couldn't understand, there seemed to be some nice pieces in both of your stuff, but who knows. yes I'm fine, they kept me over night at the hospital and when he came home at two a.m.

James found you, he was very upset, he wanted to stay here, but I wouldn't hear of it, he had to go home to his family and work and I'm here to take care of you.

Don't move, I know it hurts, you were banged up real bad Cara-Ann hun, you almost died.

Don't worry we'll figure it out together, you sleep and heal, that's all you need to worry about, mother has it well in hand." She kissed my forehead and I drifted to sleep, with her soft warm hand resting on my forehead.

It took three weeks of sleeping and healing to make it out of the hospital and home. Mother had moved my bed downstairs in the sitting room and she had made out the couch for her to sleep, this made me smile.

She would talk every night as I drifted to sleep telling me stories from her childhood and about her friends she knew today.

Some stories I had heard as a child some I had never heard, It was very soothing to me to hear her voice calmly tell her stories. I tried to stray wake to hear them but would always fall asleep quickly each night.

Slowly I mended and began to move around more, we lived downstairs, there was a full bath off the kitchen, so we avoided going up the stairs. Every time I would pass the front stairs on my way to the kitchen a shiver ran up my spine.

It took two weeks, then one day I ran upstairs to the library for a book to read without thinking about it, I tried to open mothers bedroom door but couldn't, that took another two weeks and when I did I was shocked. There was a new bed and new wallpaper, it was so beautiful I cried.

Mother found me there and held me crying with me. I couldn't tell if I was crying because we had been after mother for years to update her bedroom, or for what had happened in this one room, daddy's dieing, my rape and beating. After wards I knew one thing I had hidden enough. It was time to move on, we moved back upstairs.

Mother called Jack and he came over that day and moved my bed back upstairs, mother explained that Jack was the one who redid her bedroom, cleaning up all the blood in the process. I started to wonder if I had been wrong about him, but I wasn't in a trusting mood, so I kept my distance from him.

Chapter 07
“The Homecoming”
By Deana Rae Higgins

Sabbatical

Time moved forward fall turned to winter; Jack helped me and mother ready for it.

We winterized the truck and home. Jack chopped wood and stacked it by the kitchen door; we would need it and use it all this winter.

Time kept me so busy that I had no time to feel sorry for my self. I was working again from my home laptop, making money we needed to survive. Mother never asked and I never said it, it was just understood that I was staying home with her. My day’s of flying solo, over. I couldn’t even think about being alone or leaving mother alone, not as long as Jason was still out there.

I had not seen or heard anything about him and would not ask for fear my mother would put two and two together.

One day I caught Jack outside working and asked him to put in a security system inside and out, with cameras and an alarm. I had ordered the entire thing and had it delivered by truck soon as I returned home.

I called my friend Mary soon as I had gotten home but, she had disappeared the day of dad's funeral. Because her car had not been found the police wouldn't look for her.

I knew she was dead, Jason had told me so, but getting anyone to listen was hard as I wouldn't give up Jason. I couldn't yet.

Mother did receive a call from the county, giving her back the title to her home and a new court date to sue for the rest of the land, Mary had filed papers in court before she disappeared, thank god. I knew that the whole thing was handled wrong, but I wish I could understand what it was really about, I couldn't believe it was over land but had nothing to go on, so slowly mother and I began to relax; our home was safe for now.

With me working from home and making money things began to look up for us both. It had snowed and the white of the land around us hid any faults and soothed our hearts and minds.

Every night mother and I played scrabble after dinner, drinking hot tea and enjoying each other's company.

We made homemade bread, cakes and pies and gave them away to Jack and mothers friends as fast as we made them. Both of us so grateful to all of them for everything they had done for us both. It was a time of love, family, neighbors and peace for us.

Winter moved forward in a slow pace and we used every minute of each day to bond and enjoy life with each other and friends and family.

James came in several times alone, staying over night and once brought the whole family for a weekend visit.

Thanksgiving came and mother and I opened up the house and fed almost everyone in town, including James, his family and his wife's family.

It was so nice to have the children running and laughing thru the house, it had been so empty with just me and mother in it.

We even opened up the sitting room again; we had covered up the furniture and closed it again after the funeral.

Mother and I even took all the curtains down and washed them, only hanging them again, a week before. We took a whole week to celebrate and eat.

We invited Jack and the new preacher, Sam in town to dinner. Mother and I had started going to church, on Wednesday's and Sunday's.

Sam had been a great friend to us both, helping us gain strength every day, we did volunteer work for the church, showing us that there were worse off, then us.

On many of a Sunday, Sam took us both out for dinner after Sunday school on Sunday's, mother would beg to stay home, but I wouldn't allow it, she needed to get out as much as I needed.

It was apparent that Sam had started feeling more then friendship for me, I just wasn't ready, yet.

But I did so enjoy his company, and so did mother. I saw laughter in her smile now that had been missing for way too long.

Then it was Christmas time and we again took time to enjoy life and family. We held a huge Christmas party to celebrate life. It was a make your gift year and turned out to be so much fun, making presents for our friends and family and some of the things we received as gifts, some useful, some just funny, but fun had by all of us who gathered to share our home with us.

I had also become friends with Jack. I found mother was right, he was a really nice man, often showing up to help when mother and I need it most. Jack and I started taking walks in the evenings, and talking, about almost every thing except what had happened to me. I would not talk to anyone about it.

I had taken the time to heal my mind and I felt that I was doing a great job at hiding my fears, when it came back to bite me in the ass.

The school in town was having there anal Christmas play, the whole town always came out to support the school kids.

James and his family had come down for the week so we wanted to take the family to see it. The twins enjoyed it so much, that I think that I heard whispers from James and his wife about moving home, I turned to look at mother and she too had heard and winked at me, then it happened, I saw Jason and gave it all away.

Mother turned to look why my face had gone white and saw him and that second she knew who had hurt me and why I hadn't told. My secret was out. Mother would never allow fear to rule our life's, I knew it would have to be solved.

The nightmares started that night. Every night I would have the same dream. A repeat of what Jason had done to me. I started having trouble sleeping, and when I did, I would awake screaming.

Mother begged me to tell her what had happened to me, it took about two weeks of horrible nights before I cracked and told her the whole story.

She listened to every word without interrupting me then she held me as I cried.

She understood the cameras and the alarm system, she understood why I hadn't told, and she even understood my anger at my body reacting to Jason's when he had raped me. I had though, that somehow it meant I enjoyed it, but mother explain our body responds to sexual touch with or without our permission.

Often raped victim's feel this way, like it their fault somehow, but its not, no is no.

Mother read book after book to me, over and over, until I began to understand her meaning. I had done nothing to invite Jason to rape me; he had violated my mind, heart and body. I had tried to fight, and gotten beat up for it,

I said no, many times, I had given in when I could no longer fight him off, that was all I had done. I had told mother of why I had left home when I graduated from school.

“You should have told me, Cara-Ann, I’m your mother, don’t ever keep such secret from me again, OK.”

“Yes, mother I will.” I promised, thankful for such a wonderful mom.

“I love you mom.” I said as I hugged her. She didn’t need to tell me, I knew she did, but hearing made me feel so safe.

As winter turned to spring, life started to fall in to a peaceful way of life, I spent time with mother and her buddies, joining in on their sewing and cooking parties, falling in love with mother’s life.

One morning in March, I awoke to birds chirping and the sounds of spring all around me; a garden was needed to fill our time and cabinet’s, so we loaded up and headed to town.

Then we saw it. A huge tractor digging holes all over our land. There where holes every two foot, they were looking for something, as we drove by I saw Jason was in the tractor, driving. This time, I didn’t feel fear I felt anger.

Anger that empowered me to action. I was going to figure this out.

Winter had been a time of healing and building family ties but it was spring now and I felt refreshed and stronger then I ever been in my life, I may have been a lamb but now I was a tigress.

What was weak now was strong. Any innocents I had was gone forever, and it was time for payment. And Jason had a big bill to pay.

Time for peace was over. Time for war had begun. I looked at mother, expecting a lecture but instead she had a smile of pride that told me I was on the right path.

"Never be afraid to tell the truth Cara-Ann, it's our only defense against the world, and if you let the bad guys of this world get away with hurting you, they steal your soul away from you, along with your pride. You'll end up spending your life hiding away feeling nothing but fear."

I knew she was right, I had to find some way to make Jason pay without losing myself in the process. When I had been taken to the hospital, they did a rape kit but nothing came out of it, I could not understand why. Jason had not used any protection when he rapped me.

His DNA should have shown up, I had scratched him during the fight and bit his lip; his blood was mixed with mine.

Someone had covered for him, I was sure of it. I had to get my hands on the sheets, which the police had taken as evidence, at the time it happened.

I had called once a week to check on my friend Mary's disappearance, but nothing had been found out, her credit cards and bank, untouched, sense the day of dad's funeral, her last gas stop was two towns over, two hours before the funeral started.

Her parents had filled a missing person's report. I prayed she would be found soon.

She was. Her car was found at the bottom of shakes cannon. Burned to a crisp, with a body inside. Mary's.

The investigators felt it was an accident, that she had been running late, speeding and missed the curve.

I knew different and would prove it, Jason had told me he killed her, I would find a way to make him pay.

Chapter 08
"The Homecoming"
By Deana Rae Higgins

Bingo's new home

Mary's parents decided to bury her in their home town, up state.

It was a three hour drive, so mother and I rented a car and drove. It was nice to get away but it was on a sad note that we left.

All the way I kept thinking about what Jason had said, I told mother and we discussed it all the way, whether Jason had killed her.

We both felt he could have and may have done so but without proof we had nothing to go on.

We also decided he could have been lying about what he had done.

I told mother about meeting Mary when I first moved to

the city, we hit it off right away and became best friends. We spend a lot nights calling each other about out day's at work. Mary worked in an office with a lot of married men; she always had a funny story about one of them making a pass at her or some funny thing one of them said that day.

I worked in a small graphic design shop, so my days were boring most days, but Mary always had a story or joke to tell.

We would go to museum's and art shows on weekends, or to the park, to walk Mary's dog, named Bingo, a English pointer, a very hyper dog, who needed to run.

I wondered where he would go now; I made a mental note to ask. Mary and I had spent so much time together, she was the only thing I missed about the city and now she was gone, I would miss nothing; I had grown up and came home to stay.

Nothing would make me leave again, not Jason or anyone else.

We found the funeral home by following the directions that Mary's mom had giving us. It was a really beautiful place and very large. Mary's parents made sure there only daughter went out in high class style.

They loved her very much, it was easy to see, her six brothers had a very special place for their only sister, it was sad to see their loss.

We drove in the funeral recession in our rented car.

The final resting place for Mary was on a hill over looking a lake filled with geese. There were lilies all around of every color. If it wasn't a cemetery it would have been a great picnic place on a Sunday with your lover.

There were trees and green grass as far as the eye could see it was very well taken care of. Mary's family had a huge lot just for their family with the family name in huge letters on the iron fence that went around all the family plots. It was trilling to see such a huge family tree, dead and alive.

There was family from around the globe. It was a very large affair. Mother and I felt lost in the mist of so many, but Mary's Mom made us feel so welcome, we fit in, like we were family too.

At one time I saw mother having a nice talk with Mary's mom and dad, I wondered what was so secret but there was too much going on for me to wonder long.

I met all her brothers and family of all sorts. I met friends from school, and old boyfriends, some of whom, I heard stories about from Mary.

It was nice to see and meet so many people who loved her like I had.

We ate and visited until dusk, and then we said our goodbye's, to protest from Mary's mom about us staying the night. But we needed to go home, we had promised to help with church the next morning and there was no way I was letting Sam down, I really was starting to like him a lot.

As I readied to leave, Mary's dad brought in Bingo, I thought to say goodbye, only I wasn't the one saying goodbye, it was Mary's parents, whom said goodbye to

Bingo, he was coming home with mother and myself. I was so happy I started crying, that was the secret that the tree of them had been discussing.

"We could use some protection!" Said mother laughing as Bingo gave her a big wet kiss hello as we loaded him in the car.

"Thank you mom, I love you, you're the best." Was all I could say to her.

"No problem, you're the best too, and we could use some more protection, not to mention the company, Cara-Ann I would have liked your friend, I'm sorry that I'll only know her thru you, don't worry, we'll figure this whole thing out together, ok sweetie."

We turned the radio up and sang our way home, the three of us.

It was late when we pulled up to the house. We had stopped and had coffee several times, to keep myself awake, not that I was tired, it had been a long day but sad and happy at the same time, I knew that Mary would want me to have her dog, he had known me from the time he was a small pup so it was only right.

I had even helped in his training and kept him over night sometimes when Mary went out of town, he even ha a bed and toy's at my apartment in the city, I would have to go storage and dig them out, I had had my apartment packed and moved to a storage building, next city over when I decided to stay here, I had gone to get some of my things I needed and wanted to keep but was thinking of selling the rest.

Mother and I laughed all the way home at Bingo, hanging his head out the window. He knew he was going to a new home and he was excited about it that and riding in the car, his favorite thing to do, my new co pilot when I drove to town alone, I though.

When we pulled up we knew something was wrong, the front door was wide open, blowing in the wind, we had locked it when we left. Someone had broken in and left in a hurry.

I made mother stay in the car, with the windows and doors locked while Bingo and I looked thru the house. It was a disaster area, it looked like a twister came inside the house.

Stuff was taken out of every drawer and closet, thrown aside, beds over turned and broken dishes and whatnot's every where on the floor. Nothing had been over looked, they were looking for something, as we could find nothing missing when we cleaned up.

It took three day's to clean up every thing and put it back in its place.

In the hall whom ever it was had written on the wall with a black felt tip they had found in my graphic art box.

"Where is it? I want it, give it to me, or die hiding it!!!!" I knew the handwriting, I had read lots a love notes with that writing, mother saw my face and said one thing.

“Jason!” She knew too.

We talked and talked as we cleaned up, was it something he left behind when he raped me.

We couldn’t think of anything that we had, that could belong to Jason or anything he though belonged to him, except me.

We had called the sheriff and he had taken picture of the hall and home but nothing came of it again, I tried to tell him I knew who it was but he wouldn’t even listen to me.

Mother and I knew he wasn’t on our side, thank goodness we had brought Bingo home to live with us, he was our only true friend at this time that we could be sure of trusting.

Everyone else was on a watch list. Time would show our true friends and our enemy’s. Bingo fit in like an old friend, sleeping in the hall.

He could see both of our bedroom door’s as we slept. We felt better knowing that he would protect us and our home.

One night we woke to his barking at the downstairs kitchen door, and as we looked out we saw tail lights in the distance, hauling ass fast. We laughed knowing it was Jason coming to scare us again.

For dinner the next day Bingo had hamburgers with us like a long lost family member.

We had looked at the tapes from the camera’s and couldn’t find anything, the system had been destroyed along with the alarm, that didn't go off when the house was broken into, it was as if Jason had a map of the camera's and the code to the alarm, but only two people knew the code, not even Jack knew that, just mother and myself.

We learned later he had turned off all the power, knowing our system, it had been easy to get in unseen and unheard.

But Bingo wouldn't be so easy. I got the sheets back from my rape case and spent my time having Bingo smell them teaching him to hate Jason, that's why he went off on him coming to the house in the night, he could smell him.

When we would have company over, Jack or Sam, we would put Bingo in the other part of the house, not letting anyone get close to him, at this time it was hard to trust anyone, we could not be sure how far this deception went and until we knew what the mystery was we decided to keep Bingo to ourselves.

I couldn't believe that Sam or even Jack had any thing but good inside, as I found myself liking them both, but it was best to be safe, when one mistake could have us both killed.

Jason quit digging holes on our land, we filed a petition to have it stopped, until our court date, guess that's why he paid a visit to our home, we had angered him.

When I would drive to town, with Bingo by my side, every time we came across Jason in his truck or standing at the post office, Bingo would go crazy, scaring the hell out of Jason. He had learned very well Jason's smell and it was as if somehow Bingo knew Jason had hurt me and Bingo wanted to hurt Jason back, for me. Bingo would always give me a big wet kiss, and lay beside me after Jason sightings, his way of telling me I was safe, he would make sure, Bingo would kill or die trying for me, I knew that. Somehow I always got the feeling that the look in Bingo's eyes afterward held a look that said he knew that Jason killed his master, Mary.

Bingo had a score to settle with Jason that had nothing to do with me and everything to do with me and if Jason made one mistake, Bingo would have him and Bingo would not show fear or back down, Bingo's revenge would be Jason's down fall. Bingo would show no mercy for the killer.

Chapter 09
"The Homecoming"
By Deana Rae Higgins

Birth record?

Summer came in hot, it was the hottest summer in years, and records were broken by the heat replaced with temperatures in the 100's. Mother who couldn't handle the heat stayed home during the hot days. Daddy had put in a new heat and air unit for mother the last winter before he got sick, it had been a great year for the crops the past summer and he had made some spending money.

He had also had all the vents cleaned out, so it was nice on high allergy days to come inside.

We played cards and watched a lot of movies inside the cool living room space.

When I had the internet put in for my work I had cable put in too, mother said it was a waste of money but I found her watching it a lot, something she hadn't done before but now seemed to enjoy taking it easier.

I would walk in and catch her watching a movie daddy wouldn't have enjoyed, she was learning all about herself and coming into her own.

Even thou she missed her husband, every night in bed and hated sleeping alone without him by her side, she also learned not to miss his snoring, and was sleeping better then she had in years.

She was also learning what she liked for herself not what he had liked for her; she stopped wearing black so much.

Daddy had loved her in black and dark blue, made her eyes stand out, he always said. She bought some color, into her closet, for herself.

She had started looking younger, without the stress of taking care of daddy. She started going places at night with her friends even went on a blind date, set up one of the ladies.

She lost weight so had to replace her clothes with new ones dressing in a style that daddy may not have liked but looked so very good on her.

She started writing again, poems and short stories for the newspaper. I started a scrap book for her, which made me so proud that she was my mom.

I dated some, going on dates with Jack and Sam. Jack helped us rebuild the porch, screening it in.

We put in a new back door, the one Jason had kitchen in was never the same afterwards and made us feel unsafe. The new one was made of steel and had a huge strong lock on it.

We painted the house outside and inside and made new curtains for the whole house. When we had finished it looked like a new home. The windows all clean, the sun shined in making the whole house sunny and cheerful.

We would sit outside on our new screened porch enjoying ice tea with our many visitors who drove to see us. We played gin with them for hours watching the sun set.

Sam would visit bringing church members by to see us but most of the time he came alone. We would sit for hours talking about everything; I had never been best friends with a male before, except my brother. I told things to Sam I could tell Jack, even thou we had become close too.

Jack would come by every day to do some work, I had paid him, keeping track of every hour he worked, just because we had started dating I didn't want to take advantage of him.

I was playing my cards close to the vest making sure that we only shared friendship with both men and a cheek kiss when we said goodnight or goodbye was all I would accept from either man.

I was enjoying finding my own too just like mother.

Mother had started dating a man from church; he was a widower and had moved close to his daughter, the new mail lady, in town. I tried to tell her to see others too but she said she liked him and that was that.

I started dating Tanner, the druggist's oldest son, who had moved back in to town to help out his dad.

We had seen each other in church and remembered each other from our school days, plus with mother and his mother being friends all these years, we had spent time together outside school too.

I felt bad about seeing all three men but mother reminded me that I wasn't having sex with any of them and I deserved to have some fun.

I was out with Tanner when mother was attacked.

They didn't come in the house but, parked on the hill behind the house and started shooting out the windows.

Mother called the cops but by the time they showed up the shooter was gone. I came home to find Ben, her new friend and her at the table drinking coffee; I knew something was wrong; mother never drank coffee so late unless she wanted to stay up.

I called Jack to come board the windows up until we could replace them and he decided to move into Jacks bedroom.

It made me feel better but also made me feel trapped as he knew I was dating others beside him. It was important to that mother was safe, so I let him, with no hesitation.

We had no choice we had to let Bingo get to know him. Jack and Bingo took to each other fast, that's when I knew I could trust Jack.

If Bingo liked him no was ok.

Jack or Bingo would stay with mother at all times, she was never alone again. I didn't think that the shooter might to kill her as the windows he shot at where upstairs in dark rooms and mother was downstairs with the lights on but one could never be sure.

I was not going to lose my mother too.

We moved all of Jacks stuff into the library, hanging his hat and gown up on the wall. Jack had given up his rented room in town and moved all his stuff into our home, he didn't have much I noticed, and some how that worried me. Was he a drifter? Did he have family? I tried to get him to open up and talk about himself but he was a hard shell to crack.

This added to his charm. When I would go out with Sam or Tanner I would come home to him sitting at the kitchen table waiting for me.

Jack and I stopped dating when he moved in because one of us had to stay to protect mother.

It drove me crazy I found myself on my dates thinking about Jack. I also found I looked forward to coming home to our late night talks more fun then the dates themselves.

I started coming up with reasons to come home early or to not go at all. The tree of us would play scrabble late into the nights or mother would retire early to leave us alone where we would watch TV or movies or just talk for hours on end.

Bingo would curl up next to Jack and stay there for the whole time we talked raising his head once in a while to look at Jack or me wagging his tail. I kidded I would sue Jack for stealing the affections of my dog, but I loved it.

We settled into a happy place learning about me and finding out nothing about him, except that he loved dogs.

Then the phone calls started, late at night, hang-ups at

first, then heavy breathing.

When Jack would answer the caller would cuss at him, asking where it was. When I would answer I would hear lewd remarks. I knew it was Jason.

We decided it was time to figure out it was he wanted, Jason gave us that opportunity the next week, without us having to plan anything, just take advantage of the situation.

Mother had gone to bed early, not feeling well, she had got a cold that was tiring her out.

Jack and I were on the porch when we saw the truck coming our way, we weren't expecting any company. At first we just watched as the truck came closer in the dim light of sunset, we both figured out who it was at the same time and shouted out together.

"Jason."

He drove right up to the house and got out.

My heart started pumping so hard in my chest I was sure that Jack heard it but Jack was lost in his own world, his face turning red and a look of anger replacing his smile, his green eyes looked black. He loved us, that's why he's so mad, my mind though, making me smile, Jack turning his head saw my smile and that I was looking at him not Jason and a small quick smile came across his face his eyes flashed green then turned back to black as he turned to watch Jason walk to the back door.

"What do you want coward?" Jack asked with anger in his voice. I had never seen him angry and made a mental note never to give him a reason to have him mad at me.

"I want it!" Jason stated, his voice showing anger too, his eyes watching me. I was scared but would not let Jason see it, I had Jack to protect me and Bingo, who was standing at the screen door growing a low deep growl that made Jason reach up and put his hand on the screen door to make sure it didn't open up letting Bingo out in the yard with him.

"What is it you want Jason, we don't have anything that belongs to you, I would know if we did." Opening my mouth for the first time sense he had showed up uninvited. I surprised myself at how calm my voice was.

"Fine we'll play this game, I want the birth record, the one your dad has stashed somewhere, find it and give it to me or else." He stated calmly with no emotions at all.

"Else what?" Jack asked quickly standing up and moving to stand by Bingo and hiding me from Jason. Jason stepped back and I could see his face filled with fear, before Jack moved again hiding me.

"You'll find out, ask Cara-Ann what I can do, she'll tell you." And Jack knew who had rapped me and put me in the hospital, I hadn't told anyone but mother, so he had no knowledge of my knowing who it was.

The anger on his face must have shown cause Jason ran to his truck and jumped inside locking the door and taking off in a could of dust.

Jack had reached to open the door but stopped when Jason took off. He now dropped his arm to his side and turned to face me. His face said it all.

He was disappointed in me for not trusting him enough to tell him the truth. I tried to explain why I couldn't tell but he just walked off going upstairs leaving me sitting alone with my thoughts.

Tears ran down my cheeks as I though about how much I had hurt Jack the look of hate had been replaced with hurt and I had seen it and caused it. It would haunt my dreams.

I tried to knock on bedroom door but I knew it was best to let it be for the night.

The next morning I awoke to Jack gone, moved out in the night, I couldn't understand why? How could he leave us here when we needed him so much? Why was he so mad at me for not telling my secret to him? It was mine to tell, why the big deal?

I told mother everything that was said last night. She too couldn't understand why Jack had been so mad and she had no ideal what Jason meant when he said he wanted the birth record that dad was supposed to have hid somewhere. We dug out the big heavy bible with all the births record in it but saw nothing that would raise an eye brow.

We even searched the records at church the following Sunday but found nothing out of the ordinary or that anything everyone didn't know already.

We were watching a pirate moving on TV the next Saturday when we looked at each other and both remember at the same time. The map we had found in daddy's stuff when we cleaned out his drawers. We had given it to James.

We couldn't get to the phone fast enough to call him and have him fax it to us. He wasn't home and we left a message for him to call us, not wanting to leave such an important fact not sure about who could be listening in on our phone calls. Party line doesn't need a warrant to listen.

We could do nothing but wait, so we went to bed, I dreamed of pirates and hidden treasure. In the morning light I laughed at myself, hidden treasure, not probable, more likely nothing that means anything but at least we had something to go.

It was noon before we got in touch with James and had him fax over a copy, he had had the paper tested he said, it was over fifty years old, laughing at the though of buried treasure on our land.

We hung up, laughing with him, but mother and I knew it was no laughing matter, out lives as well as the land was at stake.

We had to figure out what it was that Jason wanted now that we were on our own again, Jack had not been seen or heard from sense he had moved out of our home, leaving us woman alone.

Thank goodness we had Bingo to watch over us and to protect us from Jason should he decide to enforce his pledge to hurt us. I had never felt so alone in my life. I had shut down my ties to Sam and Tanner.

I had no one to talk to. Slowly I started to get over Jack's leaving and Sam started coming over for dinner again. Tanner had started dating Tammy Smith, the receptionist at city hall, now I really didn't like her.

Every time I would see Tanner at the drug store I wondered if I had made the right choice. In church when I would see him sit beside Tammy, I would get jealous of her.

Mother and I spent hour after hour looking at the map but we couldn't tell where the spot that had the big red x marked was located at. So I decided to try the library for old maps of the area. I copied what I could and brought them home to look at.

The more I looked the more one thing stood out, the big old tree in the front yard, that's where the map seemed to be pointing at, but what if we dug up the tree and it was nothing, it would be a shame to loss such a old friend.

The tall oak tree that stood for a hundred years, that dad had played on as a child, which James and I played on and would swing on in our tire swing.

We would have to do some hard thinking…

Chapter 10
"The Homecoming"
By Deana Rae Higgins

This time, I win

Mother and I talked for hours but there was no way we could kill the oak tree out front, no matter what trash Jason was trying to sell us.

Sometimes it best to wait and see and that's what we decided to do, wait.

It was late summer and I had been home a year, so we decided to visit dad's grave, we hadn't been in a while and it was almost his year anniversary too.

The grave and headstone looked in great shape and well taken care of. We put new flowers and after a spell I walk over to the church wall and waited, I could still see her but was out of earshot.

Mother had some things she needed to talk to dad about

alone; she was getting serious about Bob, the hardware owner and an old friend of dad's. It was just one of those things, she went with me one day for some things for the house and they started talking and have been ever sense.

She didn't want to betray daddy but she also didn't want to spend the rest of her life alone.

I had taken over the work around the house, and our court date had been set for late fall, so she was free to do what pleased her.

I had watched mother come into her own the last year and it was like watching a butterfly emerge.

We grabbed dinner at the only diner in town and I dropped her at Bob's house, they needed to talk about their future, I had given my blessings.

Mother had never kissed anyone but my dad until the other night when Bob brought her home after a date. It made her feel like a teenager, she said, yet it felt wrong.

"Mother daddy would not want you to live your life for him, he's gone mother he's not coming back, it's not like he went to the store. You have to go on, it's what makes life worth living, and Bob's really nice and he respect dad, what more could you want.

Friendship that has turned to love and need, and YOU said he made your toes curl up when he kissed you. Mother I'm here to stay, you don't have to worry about me or take care of me. I'm a big girl, I can take care of myself and I have Bingo mother."

I had my say and left it up to her to decide what to do,

which is why we went to see dad's grave, I hoped what ever she decided to tell Bob was good news.

Mother deserved to be happy, life is too short, not to be.

I was happy when she called to say that she was staying the night with Bob talking, knowing mother that was all they would be doing. I laughed thinking of poor Bob working so hard to get in my mom's pants, hope he was up for the challenge.

Mother could use some love in her life and man in her bed I though. Then I laughed out loud making Bingo lift his head, turning it sideways to look at me like I had lost my mind.

"I should take my own advise, huh Bingo, come on lets go to bed, baby."

We crawled in bed, me in mine and Bingo in his. We drifted to dream land, his of big bones and bird's to chase, me of flowers and crop's growing in the fields.

I heard a loud bang. Bingo went downstairs to investigate it and I drifted back to sleep. I awoke next to Bingo barking at my bedroom door and growling, at first I couldn't comprehend what was going on, then I remembered I hadn't shut my bedroom door, had the wind, I sat up, trying to see in the dark, I could not.

Bingo was going off like I was in danger, then it dawned on me that the only person Bingo hated that much was Jason. I sprang out of bed to go open my bedroom door, I never made it, I ran right into Jason's fist, knocking me out cold.

When I came to, I was tied up, my hands above my head and my legs spread eagle, tied apart, I was nude. I wasn't home I could tell I could see nothing in the dark or hear anything for that matter, not even Bingo.

"Please God, let Bingo be ok." I whispered in the dark.

"Oh he is, he's waiting for your mom to come home. Jason whispered.

"Yep he'll be just fine." He continued as he flipped on the over head light, a bare bulb, very bright, so bright I had to shut my eyes for a second, I opened them to see Jason staring at my nude body.

"Yep, always did love your sexy body Cara hun, I could look at you all day, ah now don't be ugly, your mine honey and I want you to want me the way I want you."

He whispered as he ran his hand up and down my body touching me with his fingertips very softly, making my body respond to his touch, I tried to move, to turn away, but I couldn't, I could only move my head in shame, hiding my eyes as the tears started to fall.

"Haha, see baby your body loves me and in time so will you, you see baby I'm going to make love to you until your body loves me and only me, so it will respond to me and only me."

"NO! I screamed loud as I could.

"Help me please, help me, fire, help" I yelled,

remembering that experts tell you to yell fire when you're being raped to draw help faster.

"Go ahead baby yell all you want, I want you to be vocal, if fact you yell out all you want, when I'm making sweet love to you. Cara I've loved you my whole life I've never loved anyone the way I love you, I don't even enjoy having sex with any woman but you, believe me I tried, but none of them whore's here in town are good enough to wipe your boots, baby.

Now, now, clam down, fells good huh baby, me touching you, your shin is so soft baby. I'm sorry that I have to keep you tied up I so wish you would just relax and go with it, I'm the best lover you will ever have, or am I the only lover you ever had. Am I baby? My God I am! Your face tells me everything I need to know, damn it hun, I'm so happy.

"You've made your daddy very happy baby.

I'm going to teach you all the fine arts of love making then we will learn to great joys of wild sex. SHHH baby its ok, no crying, unless it's happy tears. Right here baby, see how your body responds to my touching you here. That's it baby, move with it, let it take over your whole body,

I'm going to make you have the best organism ever, you will want and need me for pleasure, just wait, Oh yes baby feel that. That's it, that's it, see baby, come on baby, oh yes scream for me, yes that's it. Reach for it baby, that's it come for daddy, oh baby yes, I knew you would like it, baby daddy is always going to take care of your needs, no one will ever satisfy you like I do, look at how much your nipple's love my touch, you like that hun baby, want me to pinch it hard for you, oh yes, I knew you like it ruff, my baby girl, oh yes. Not its time for daddy to get his nuts off, ready baby, your nice and hot, huh baby.

Oh yes keep yelling keep pretending you don't like it, I like the virgin act, your body tells me different baby, that's it rock with me, yes rock baby, move your fine bod, ohhhhh yes come with me baby, you are going to have my baby."

I tried to control my body but again it betrayed me, enjoying Jason touch, his kisses on my nipples, making them hard, wanting him. I hated Jason and I hated myself even more, I felt so ashamed of myself, how could I respond to his touch.

His baby, I would die first, I would jump off the bridge. There was no way I was going to carry his demon child. I had never taken birth control, as there was no reason too, I prayed that I would not get pregnant with his child, he was right about one thing, I had only been with Jason, just never found anyone I wanted to, yet, I wish I had made a pass at someone, I hated the smirk that Jason got form the knowledge that I had only been with him.

When Jason had finished he turned out the light and left shutting the door behind him, leaving me to cry in the dark, I felt so ashamed of myself. I cried myself to sleep as best I could, my hands had begun to hurt from being tied above my head, they eventually went numb and I was able to doze lightly.

Later in the day Jason came back and untie my hands,

keeping my feet tied, I tried to get him to trust me to let my feet go and not tie my hands, but he wouldn't talk to me, he just brought in a bucket and some food and water on a tray and left.

Could he feel guilty, I wondered, maybe I could work on that, I untied my legs and got up, unsteady at first, but at least I could move around, I used the bucket and ate the food and drank all the water, then I began to bang on the door yelling as loud as I could, praying someone would hear me.

I did this for about five minutes, then I started to feel funny, woozy, like I was drunk, I stumbled to the bed, Jason had drugged me, what a ass was my last though as I passed out.

Jason held me this way for three months, making my mother frantic over my disappearance.

He would visit me, sometimes he would talk, and I would wake up tied up hearing his voice telling me how much he loved me and how sorry he was that I made him do it this way. Why couldn't I understand we belonged together he would shout at me, slapping my face, until I would come to.

Other times I would wake to my body responding to his touch, I would try to stop him, to push him away but I was so drugged I couldn't hardly move at times. I asked what was it, he was giving me, but he laughed and said it's to make you love me hun, I'm retrain your body and mind to love me.

"The drugged you, is the real you Cara, feel it, let go of yourself, baby."

I drifted between this world and the drugged world, sometimes not knowing which was which, or how much was real or dreams.

One morning Jason woke me to get up and pee, I was so doped up he had to hold me up and walk me to sit on the bucket, I noticed he held a stick between my legs, a pregnancy's test,

I knew then he would not let me go until I was pregnant. Each time it would come back negative he would slap me hard across my face and body, rapping me with an animal lust, yelling over and over, make it a boy baby, a boy.

Over and over he did this, coming in to see me in between to talk or make slow love to me making my body betray me over and over.

Then one day the stick came back positive and Jason was very sweet and gentle with me. He held me, rocking me, feeding and stopped drugging me, thank God.

My head began to clear and my mind started planning my escape from Jason's hell, I wouldn't allow myself to think about the baby growing inside me, I couldn't yet, that would have to wait, maybe I prayed it's a mistake.

Every day my body and mind became stronger and I watched everything Jason did waiting for my move to escape from him.

He would still hit me if I tried to move to fast or upset him in any way, so I had to be careful, I didn't want to lose the baby in front of him, no telling what he would do in his anger, maybe even kill me.

He would come in and make me lay down as he tied me up, holding me, talking to me, begging me to love him back, I would try to say the words to go along with him but the words would not come out of my mouth. He knew I didn't because he would still have to tie me up to rape me over and ever, I would not let him, no matter what my body responded to his touch or how much it betrayed me, my mind hated him and my mind controlled me.

I would lay in wait just waiting for the day I could break away from him.

"Where is it?" He would ask over and over at first. I must have told him during one of my drugged states, because he stopped asking after a while and seemed to feel we had become closer for my truth.

Then he made his mistake, he came in drunk one night wanting to get lovie dovie with me, I played along until I could make my move.

I felt his body slump next to the wall, sliding off of me, giving me just enough room to jump up, off the bed, he tried to catch me with his hands but I moved back and his hands grabbed at air missing me, I grabbed the bucket and swing at him hitting in the head, he swayed a bit then started after me.

I hit him again and again swinging the bucket with all my might, it was metal bucket so I know that it hurt when I hit him.

He just stood there not moving forward or backwards just looking at me with each hit, his eyes filled with hatred, swaying a little side to side when I would hit him, blood was running down the side of his face where I had hit him.

I knew that if I didn't escape now he would kill me for sure.

I swung with all my might catching Jason on the side of his head, beside his left eye, blood spurted out as the bucket met flesh and bone. He rocked back and I hit him again and again and again.

I saw the light leave his eyes and he feel backwards hitting the floor hard, banging the back of his head on the concrete floor, I ran out, shutting the door behind ,and locking it, just in case he woke up before I could get help. I didn't think he was dead, just passed out from my hitting him and from being drunk.

I ran outside but I was in the country and no other house could be seen, I looked around remembering where I was, It was what used to be the widow Johnson place, it was very rundown and looked as if Jason had been living here a while, I saw his truck and ran to it, the keys hung from the ignition, how lucky could I be, I had not wanted to go back inside to look for them.

I drove myself to the emergency room, parked Jasons truck and walked in.

"May I help you?" The young nurse asked very sweetly and soft, looking me over, seeing my black eyes and dried blood on my face.

"I been held hostage and raped, help me please." Then I fainted, I came to in a private room.

There was a nurse standing beside me as the doctor stood to the side talking on his cell phone.

This time I had Jason, his DNA was all over me and in me, I had the doctor do a pregnancy test, along with the AIDS test they did. She, the doctor examined me, head to toe, gave me a stitch on the cut on my head, and sent for the cops.

"Who did this Cara-Ann?" They asked.

"Jason Black, he can be found at widow Johnson place." Was all I said, as I laid back on the bed, I had him this time, he was going to prison.

Chapter 11
"The Homecoming"
By Deana Rae Higgins

I woke up in love

I woke up this morning, loving myself and life for the first time a long time. A heavy burden had been lifted from my shoulders, Jason had been arrested and charged with kidnapping and rape, he was not going to get off this time, his buddies at town hall would not be able to pull any stunts, at least I believed so.

Mother had come to the hospital to pick me up, the look on her face said how proud she was of me, and I had not hidden this time, not from fear or shame. I couldn't, I just didn't know how to tell her yet, but it was a secret I wouldn't keep long, as my morning sickness would tell her she need to know soon.

As I lay there day after day waiting to escape from Jason I spend time thinking that it was wrong to make an innocent baby pay for who he, or she‘s, father was, and with Jason in jail, I would keep him out of the picture for good.

At first mother and I really didn’t talk about what happened to me, and the horrible things that Jason did to me, in the name in of love.

Slowly I started to open up and when I told her what Jason had done to me, including the baby, first she got mad, then sad then very happy.

“A grandchild, oh how wonderful. We are happy right?” She asked unsure of how I felt about it, reading my face.

“Yes mother we are very happy, and it doesn’t matter how this child was conceived we are going to raise him or her with love.

A baby in the house, my baby, I had so much love to share, and I would do what ever I needed to do to protect my child.

From the minute I found out that Jason had got what he wanted, I knew that I would change his plans, I would keep this baby but I would lose him forever, my child will not ever know who his or her father was.

Mother was so happy about being a grandmother again and because she had the twins, both girls, she wanted a grandson, I had to admit a boy sounded nice but then so did a girl.

All the test that the hospital did came back good and it felt right to keep the baby. Not that I could have terminated my pregnancy.

It was something I couldn't do plus I felt maybe I was ready for a child, I didn't have a man in my life now so it wasn't going to be a problem there, and with working at home I could make money thru the whole pregnancy, so that wouldn't be a problem either and with mom's help, I felt I could do this alone.

Jason's court date came and I had to go testify for the prosecutor. It was extremely hard to tell what happened to me in front of people and Jason but I made myself do it.

Mother came with me every day and sat in the courthouse listening to my horror tails of Jason raping me and all the terrible things he said and did.

I did not tell them I was pregnant even thou the doctor knew and when she took the stand she let it slip so the court made me take a DNA test to see if Jason was the father as proof of his rape and of course it came back his by DNA, I would make sure that he was never my child's father.

The doctor told of my shock when I came into the emergency room and of my cuts and bruises.

They had huge pictures that had been taken at the hospital showing my black eyes, they even had me testify about Jason hitting me and almost killing me the first time, bring in my hospital records from that time too. I told it all even of how I left home because of his jealous behavior.

I told of his hitting me back then too, things I never told my mom or anyone else.

I told of how he said he killed my friend Mary and how he told me he would kill my mother if I went against him. I told all Jason's dirty little secrets that he made me keep in shame and fear.

Then a funny thing happened I started holding head high again and pride return to my heart for myself. And fear became replace with strength to stand tall and to stop being a victim, I was done wrong not the other way around, and I would make sure my child never felt any thing but love for how his or her came into my life and this world.

Jason was found guilty, it took the jury ten minutes to decided and most of that time was walking time in and out of the jury room, because the room was located at the back of the court house.

He was given life in prison, when he heard the news he jumped up and started screaming at me.

"You will pay for this Cara-Ann, as my child grows inside you, you will know the mistake you made, I know you love me Cara-Ann, I know it, and I will come for you and my baby…"

It was the last thing I heard as they took him from court in handcuffs and chains around his ankles, it was a sight I totally enjoyed seeing on him.

As he walked a look of pain would cross his face and I wanted to see more pain in fact I hated Jason so I wanted him dead but I was glad I had only slightly hurt him when I escaped from his prison but I knew that if he ever came near me or my child again I would not hesitate to kill him.

Coming near us or even trying to have anything to do with us was a death sentence for sure.

The court had ordered him not to have any contact with me or my unborn child, his rights, if he had any, were dissolved in court that day too.

I wanted nothing more from him he had giving me everything I needed or could handle from him. My life would never be the same and I felt that I wouldn't be able to trust any man or even fall in love ever again.

I wouldn't even talk to Sam or Tanner and they both tried to reach me after I came home the second time from the hospital.

I had no time for love and felt my heart had harden against men, the funny thing I didn't know if I liked it this way or not, I was very confused. I had a baby to think about and I made my life around that, mother and working on the farm.

The court's dates for the land and came by too and we had won.

All of our land was given back to mother, and the city was fined for taken our land in the first place and the court ordered them to pay mother so that mother had some money of her own to spend on herself, she spent most on the house and land, buying seed and fertilizer and fixing the tractor so that we could plaint crops.

We hired some young men from town to help us with the hard stuff, with me pregnant, I could do any heavy lifting.

At first mother and I though it would be hard to run a farm, just two woman but turned out we loved being the boss' and being charge.

Mother took to it so well I felt daddy had missed out on so much by not having mother help him, he never got to see the woman that I saw; she was strong, smart and one tuff cookie.

He missed out on so much by making her weak and keeping her in the house, I couldn't help think maybe if he had let her help him maybe stress wouldn't have killed him so early in his life.

Mother didn't stress over the farm like dad did, she just did what was needed and let it go. But maybe almost losing it all made her stronger.

Mother had a feel for what was important and what was not. We worked and spent time enjoying life together as my belly grew bigger every day.

I had started having Sam over for dinner at times as friends, he understood that anything else was out of the picture for no and maybe forever.

Mother continued to see Bob, even thou for a while she stopped; I convinced her she had nothing to fell bad about. If she been there that night Jason could have hurt her, maybe even killed her.

If Bingo was out smarted by Jason, he could have and would have hurt mother so I was glad she wasn't home that night.

Poor Bingo followed me everywhere I went, he knew he had made a mistake that night and was not going to let it happen again.

As the baby grew inside me he would lay his head

against my belly and I felt sure he could hear the heartbeat, I even asked Bingo once if I was having a boy or girl and he seemed to fell it was boy, mother and I had a huge laugh over a dog who could tell you the sex of your baby, while still unborn, we could get rich, taken him on all the talk shows, showing off his skills.

It was so fun to see Bingo bond with the baby, before its birth.

We didn't get much money from the crops because of it being so late in the season, but we did get some canned goods that we kept and some we passed on to the neighbors.

We felt so good about following in daddy's footsteps about sharing and caring for our neighbors, fall was coming in cool with long lazy day's, so we spent our time doing work for the church and mother spend most of her nights at Bob's.

I kidded her that she should just move in with him but mother was taking her time, she didn't feel right living in sin she said and one marriage was enough for her.

My baby was due the first of April, I still had six months to prepare for my child's birth, and I chose to turn James room into a nursery for the baby. It was close to my room and James wouldn't need it. I removed the bed and left the dresser, it was a huge heavy one and I like it. It would hold a lot of the baby's stuff and with a little work really looked nice.

I decided to wait until I knew the sex to paint, I could have found out when they did the DNA test but I didn't want to know, so it was left unanswered.

I felt that Jason had no right to know weather he had a boy or girl.

Mother spoiled me so much during this time, we truly learned so much about each other that we had never taken the time to learn before.

We joined a book club and we would read to each other out loud. That way the baby could hear the books too.

When mother would come across a cuss word or a seine she though was to grownup for the baby she would spell out the words or whisper the words, it was so funny to see mother so happy.

Mother had decided to marry Bob after all and had set the day for the twelve of December, so had a weeding to plan too. She couldn't stay away from Bob any more, he treated her so good that mother, mother couldn't continue to hurt his feeling's anymore.

That's when I knew she love Bob and he loved her more than anything.

It wasn't that daddy didn't love mother, he loved

her and took great care of her, he just didn't let her be herself and Bob lets her be herself not whom he wants, she started working at the drug store with Bob and had taken over the books and was doing a great job for him.

Mother said she was having so much fun, a paycheck was icing on the cake. She had even learned to drive and bough herself a new car with the money she won.

To see mother drive out to the farm and around town was the coolest thing. Bob taught her to drive his car, because he said she needed to learn to take care of herself. She was a grown woman very capable of learning to drive a car.

He also made her open a bank account in her name alone for the farm monies she made.

He gave her the convenience to become the woman she had always dreamed of becoming, the woman she always expected me to be.

I watched in aw of the woman she became. I had always had so much respect for my parents but watching mother made me so proud of her.

I spent every minute I could helping her plan her wedding, it was to be a small affair in the church that daddy was buried behind but I thought he would like the man she feel in love with and planed to marry.

They had been friends after all for years. I figured out that Bob had a thing for my mother for years but would never had said any thing to either of my parents.

This made me smile to know my mother had been loved in secret for her whole life, I knew Bob would never do anything to hurt my mother and would spoil her the rest of her life, like she deserved to be.

We had forgot about the supposed treasure under the old oat tree out front, it didn't matter to us in the mist of everything else going on. Mother and I both seemed so happy as we moved closer to her wedding date, we didn't waste any time thinking about it.

Until James came home for thanksgiving. He had had the map analyzed by experts at the university in his state. We knew it was very old paper, but what he found out, made us decide we had to figure out what it was that someone wanted and just who this someone was.

Written across the map in concealed ink was the numbers 23-46-19-17- the expert though it was a code to a lock of some kind.

The mystery of the treasure map was driving me crazy, so with James' help we started the hunt to solve it, what we found, left us all in shock for a long ,long time, and we found out things we had never known or could even dream of in our wildest dreams.

Chapter 12
"The Homecoming"
By Deana Rae Higgins

Handyman for hire

Mother's wedding came off without a hitch, every thing was so beautiful.

Mother's dress was made of old lace and was a soft cream color, it may have been whiter at one time but with age it had darken some.

We found it at an antique store in the next town, it fir her like it was made just for her. Bob wore his old tux; he had had for years it fit right in.

It was a small affair with mom and Bob's friends and James family and me. We held it inside the front room with mother coming down the stairs I couldn't remember when she had looked so pretty or so happy.

Mother loved daddy very much and he her but Bob made the light in her eyes shine and for that I was very thankful. Even James and his wife Carrie saw what I saw, and we three decided we liked it a lot.

We held a reception after and then the happy couple left to Bob's house, they couldn't afford to take time off from work for a real honeymoon but it didn't seem to matter to them.

Mother had moved some of her things and gave the rest to me, farm and all.

James, Carrie and the twins stayed with me for Christmas, but I knew after that I would be alone and needed help so I put a ad in the county paper for a handyman to help around the farm, it was winter but there was a lot of work that needed done and only me to do it, I needed help.

With mother's money from the settlement we fixed up the barn and put in a small apartment up top, for such a reason.

I put the ad in the paper the middle of December I received no calls until around the sixth of January.

Christmas had come and gone. It was a wonderful time for all of us including mom's new husband Bob and his daughter and husband from out of state with their daughter, who happened to be the same age as the twins. They became best friends at once.

At first Bingo and I rumbled around the house lost. But we settled into a nice routine that fits us.

With the baby coming, I decided to make James room the baby's and mothers a sitting room. I put in a couch, rocking chair, television and small refrigerator for my drinks and the baby's bottles.

It was just perfect for the baby and me. I couldn't sleep in mothers and dad's bedroom with what had happened in there but it made a really nice upstairs room for us, a family room of sorts on the plus side it would be nice to not have to run up and down the stairs for every little thing.

The ad had been in the paper for a month now and I figured that I would have to go it alone, when one morning I was sitting outside when I saw an old pickup coming down the long dusty road that led to the farm and only mine so I knew it was company for me.

"Hope it's some help for us, huh Bingo, we sure could use some, huh boy." I said as I ran my hand across his back making his tail wag so hard his whole body moved with each wag.

I couldn't see who it was, a man with a cowboy hat on, he pulled up in a old dodge that had seen many hard times, a hard working truck for a hard working man, I hoped.

He jumped out and something about the way he moved reminded me of someone, I started to back up in fear and Bingo had started to growl under his breath stopping the man from walking and lift his head and hat giving a full view of his face, it was the most beautiful green eyes I had ever seen, it was Jack.

"Jack!" Was all I got out before I had to grab Bingo's collar to stop him from running to Jack. Both of us recognizing the man who stood before us.

"No Bingo, sit, good boy. Jack what are you doing here?"

"Hi Cara-Ann, hi Bingo." Jack smiled sweetly, walking with his hand out stretched for Bingo to smell.

He couldn't see my belly at first because of the heavy coat I had on. It was cold that day and one of daddy's old coat so it covered me up well.

"Where the hell did you disappear to Jack? I screamed making Bingo ears stand up.

"No need to upset Bingo, can we talk, please, I promise I'll tell you everything, and if you want me to go after that I will."

"We'll see, come on, I'll make us some coffee." I turned and headed into the house with Jack following me with Bingo staying in between us just in case.
Bingo wasn't sure about Jack yet, neither was I.

It was still cold in the house I like to save on my heating bill, I turned it up as I walked by but for now I keep my coat on, I hadn't decided if I wanted Jack to know I was pregnant with Jason's baby.

I made some hot coffee and cut some coffee cake and sat a piece in front of us both along with two steaming hot cups of strong coffee, I didn't drink as much with the baby on board, but one cup wouldn't hurt.
I sat looking at Jack over my cup as he devoured the

cake, like he hadn't had any thing to eat in day's, I slid over my piece and he ate that too.

Then he slowly drank his coffee looking at me over the top of his cup, drinking it all. I rose to refill both cups as he started to slowly talk.

"I'm sorry Cara-Ann about leaving, it's just, well when you didn't tell me, it reminded me of something I though I had under control, it set me off and I needed time.

I sat down, not saying anything, what ever it was, must have hurt him bad and he needed to get it off his heart and I needed to hear it.

"I was married once, we married when we were young, barely twenty-two for us both. We had been in love for years, grew up together, the whole thing, like you and Jason."

When he said Jason's name both Bingo and I growled under our breath making Jack looked at us both and frowned, realizing that Bingo knew Jason.

"She was my world, my life, my everything, I lived for her happiness."

Stopping with a sign, taking a deep breath and contending on with his story which had me all ears.

"I worked as a mechanic all day at an auto body shop in town. She was a teacher at the local high school she taught tenth grade math. She had gone to night school to get her teaching degree, I was so proud of her; she would spend all summer going to college for her masters degree."

Stopping to drink some of his coffee and wipe a tear off his cheek, trying not to let me see, I pretended I hadn't and rose to get more coffee giving him a second to recoup.

"She loved teaching, it was her dream and I loved her. I worried about some of them kids at school but she told me not to worry that she would be fine, she wasn't. I got a call one day from her school telling me she had been hurt at school and was taken to the hospital. I rushed over. I found her in the emergency room, she had been beating and raped by three of her students." At this I gasped and he stopped to look at me.

"Cara-Ann are you ok?" He asked as I rose and ran from the room to the bathroom.

"I'm fine, just need to pee I shouted back." But I wasn't. My heart had started racing and I felt sick to my stomach. I splashed cold water on my face until I felt my heart slow down and the nausea subside. I took a deep breath dried off my face and returned.

"You ok?" Jack asked as I took my seat, still wearing dad's coat not letting on I was pregnant. Shaking my head yes he returned to his story.

"She was pregnant with our first child; she lost the baby and any chance of any future babies. She blamed me for not protecting her, she didn't say it no, but I saw it in her eyes. I blamed myself too, I took time off from work all I could to take care of her, but even with her check from the school

I had to go back to work, we needed the money."

"Jack it wasn't…" I started to say but he cut me off

"I know what you're going to say, but it was my fault, she was the love of my life and I let her down. After that she sat around all day sad and depressed. I took her to doctor after doctor but she wasn't getting any better. She wouldn't let me touch her in any way. She pulled away from me crawling into herself. She closed herself off to me and all her friends.
She sat home, never leaving the house, locking the doors and windows."
"I need to get to the bathroom now, all that coffee just runs thru you." but I could tell he needed a minute alone to gather himself.

"How about another cup then?" I asked, making him laugh.

"Sure, why not." he laughed

When he returned he was calmer then before.

"After I went back to work I came home at lunch time to check on her, every day. She would be sitting in the dark, in a dazed state every day. Then one day she seemed better and the next even better, I tough she was on the mend. She had started drinking whiskey behind my back; I never knew she was doing it. I started thinking that maybe everything would work out, I told her we would adopt as many children as she wanted to but she said she wasn't ready to talk about that yet, so I let it go."

“She started dressing again and even started going outside again to do yard work. We had filled charges against all three boys and the school for not protecting her better. The court dates were very hard on her and I would take off work to go with her. At first all three boys, who turned out to be seventeen years old, were held in juvenile hall with no bond. Then they let them out on bond and everything changed, she went back to hiding, and I started calling in sick to stay home with her. I just couldn’t leave her alone. I felt so bad over not being there for her the first time, with them out, I couldn’t leave. It didn’t help thou, she hardly acknowledged that I was even there. She lived in her own world now and I couldn’t reach her. I was so angry I wanted to kill all three boys, but I knew that would help her. So I held it all in as best I could. I lost my job, but we managed on what Sara, that was my wife’s name, got from the school.”

“How about some more of that great coffee huh?” I got up to make another cup turning my back to him to give me and him a minute to collect ourselves, waiting for the coffee to make and filling the cups before I turned and sat down again ready to listen to more, my anger at Jack gone, what ever his reason for leaving it was a just one I could now see.

Even Bingo had become his friend lying at his and my feet, sleeping.

“Sara couldn’t accept the fact that the three boys were walking the streets when they had killed our baby. Then when the charges got dropped to rape only, the baby forgot, the fact that she would never be pregnant again forgot, the beating forgot and the boys receiving only probation, well she just snapped. The boys turned out to have rich parents who bought the kids out of trouble; well the whole thing was a slap in the face. I begged her to move, out of that city out of that state but she wouldn't budge."

"She wouldn't hear of moving away from our dream home. She stayed in side growing more and more depressed again. Then one day again she got up with a smile and that was the end of it, or so I thought. I started looking for work and found a job at a local rental car place, it was across town and I couldn't come home for lunch but Sara said it was fine and I believed her." His voice cracked and he had to stop for a second before he could return to talking.

"She was so up and I didn't know, how was I supposed to know, I was alone and I had no help and she shut me out…" And the tears started flowing. I got up grabbed the box of tissue's on the counter and handed it to him.

When at last he could continue he spoke very softly like the words he said were poison.

"She killed herself Cara-Ann. I came home one day to her in the bath tub, she had slit her wrists open from wrist to elbow, the water she sat in a deep red, she was as white as a ghost, I knew she was dead, right away, I've seen enough farm animals dead to know what dead looked liked. I buried her in that town under a huge oak tree sold the house and left, never allowing myself to deal with anything that happened.

Then when you got raped and didn't say anything, well it

hit me hard, that I hadn't protected you. I'm so sorry I really didn't mean to hurt you, will you please forgive me. You don't have to hire me but at least let me help you find you someone to help you, I heard about your mom and Bob and I think its so great but even with ole Bingo here you need some help and protection. What about Jason has he decided to leave you alone?"

I decided that I best tell him about what happened first, I was getting hot in dad's coat and I couldn't keep it on forever.

"Jason is at the prison for kidnapping, rape and assault, he got life. He kidnapped me and held me for three months before I escaped from him."

Jacked gasped and reached out to touch my hands, I grabbed his and held on.

"There's more Jack, I'm pregnant with his child." I stood up and took off dad's coat showing my belly to him for the first time. I couldn't get rid of my baby Jack, I was already two months along when I got away, he or she is what gave me the fight to fight my way out of that hell hole. I had to attack Jason to get out and I testified to put him away, this is my baby."

"That's why I put the ad in the paper, my child is due this spring and I will need help with the farm, did I tell you we won that case too and got back all the farm land, the whole thing was a sham from the start, them bigwigs even had to pay mom back for her money loss. It was so sweet…"

And then he kissed me, pulling me to him, and softly kissing my lips then when I melted into his arms he kissed me harder, darting his tongue inside my mouth teasing me with his. I pulled myself tighter into his body returning his kiss with my own no hesitation on my part or his.

Then he stopped pulled back looking into my face and crushed me to his chest as huge sobs of tears fell from both of us. We stood that way for what seemed like hours but was in realty only minutes.

"So I guess I can the ad out of the paper huh, seems like the job is filled. You are staying right? I asked a little unsure of what had just happened.

"Yes baby." He mouthed as he pulled me close, kissing me again and again until I could not think any more.

"That is if you want me to stay, Cara-Ann. Do you?"

I grabbed him and pulled him to me planting a deep soulful kiss, knowing full well he understood that I did, I then pulled him up the stairs as I kissed him, almost tripping.

But Jack caught me never letting my lips leave him as we drifted upstairs on what seemed like a cloud, our feet not touching the floor to my room to my bed, where we made love for the first time slowly, careful not to hurt my baby, our baby Jack called her or him as he stroked my belly feeling the baby move for the first time, ours was the last thing I heard as I drifted to sleep in Jacks arms, happy for the fist time in my life and very much in love with Jack.

Chapter 13
"The Homecoming"
By Deana Rae Higgins

Happiness comes my way

The next morning I woke refreshed, it was the best sleep I had slept in ages. I rolled over and felt empty bed. At first I got a little scared but then I could hear him downstairs talking to Bingo.

I jumped up and ran downstairs happy as a clam. I stopped at the kitchen door to watch, unseen for a second. Jack and Bingo were laughing and talking, well Jack was laughing and talking and Bingo whimpered every so often to say he understood.

I walked in; the smell was heaven and the coffee fresh. Jack had made breakfast for us.

"Good morning darlin!" He said with a huge smile on his face.

"Good morning my men, how are we this morning?"

Patting Bingo on the head as I hugged Jack.

Jack reached down and stroked the side of my face softly, then held me as he kissed me first soft and sweet then with a passion I had never felt before last night. Jack then wrapped his strong arms around me incasing me in his warmth and strength, holding me tight for the longest time. I held him right back standing there felling happiness and security for the first time in my life.

When at last he let me go my legs wouldn't hold me, they had turned to jelly, I held on to him until I could set down. The whole time Jack was laughing so hard he had tears running down his check.

"Ah baby I love how I make your knees go week" He got out between snorts of laughter.

"Feed me you big brute, me and baby JR here are hungry." I said back in laughter.

Bingo just flopped on the floor looking at us both, wagging his tail back and forth hitting the tile floor hard making a kathump sound every time it hit.

Jack had made pancakes, bacon and scrambled eggs. My favorite, he also had a pot of hot steaming coffee. I ate without a word, Jack sit down besides me and watched me the whole time with a look of pure love and happiness. It was a look that looked good on his tan face and his green eyes seemed to shine a light green. As I ate I watched his face too.

"Better?" Jack asked when I had eaten every scrap of

food on my plate.

"Yes, so much so in so many ways, very content, very." I smiled and said softy.

As he cleaned up the kitchen I watched his every move, the way his muscles moved under his tee shirt straining to get lose. The way his jeans tightened on his ass when he reached to put up the clean dishes. It was a show I was enjoying very much, when he turned and gave me a silly frown that made me laugh so hard I ran to the bathroom.

As I ran I could hear jack laughing, telling me serve's ya right. I had loved his Texan accent from the start; I just didn't want to admit how much, I wasn't scared now to show him. I came back into the room, walked by him staying my hips, rubbing against his side as I pasted him, turning to face him hooking my finger into a follow me sigh and ran for the stairs.

It took one second for Jack to understand, running after me up the stairs. We spend the morning back in bed making sweet love and talking about everything. We wanted no more secrets between us. Jason had done his damage but we came thru it better then ever, friends first now lovers.

I fell asleep in his arms again not realizing how tired I must have been, Jack held me as I slept, not sleeping himself, just holding me as I did.

"I love you Cara-Ann with all my heart, no one will hurt you again."

Was the last thing I heard as I fell asleep.

At last when I awoke, we made love again sweet and

slow.

"I love you too Jack, always have." I whispered when we had brought pleasure to each other, Jack just held me, rocking me.

At last we got up and as Jack went out side to do some work I called my mother and invited her and Bob to dinner, not explaining what it was, just that I had a surprise.

I put on my apron and started cooking my first meal as Jacks lover. We hadn't talked about marriage and I didn't want to seem needy so I hadn't brought it up either. We would just enjoy being lovers for now.

I made all of Jacks favorite's that I could remember he liked. I cooked most of the day as Jack worked outside, when he would take a time out to come in, my heart would start to beat fast, from the love I felt for him. And the look in his eyes said the same thing to me.

Every time he came in he would hold me and kiss me like we would never see each other again. His kisses left me out of breath and his touch sent shiver's up and down my spine. A feeling I tough would never come my way.

Each time before he went back outside he would kiss my belly and say goodbye to JR. in my heart I felt that Jack would be the best father for my unborn child, and each time a few tears would fall across my check when he left to go outside.

Bingo stayed awhile with me but most of the time he ran outside with Jack to see what he was up too. It made me laugh to see how happy even Bingo was, Jacks coming back was the best thing for all three of us.

It was the end of January and a hard snow had started to fall, so we decided to light up the fireplace and open up the other side of the house for our dinner with mom and Bob.

As we dusted and picked up the covers on the furniture we came up with a wonderful ideal for the farm, turn in into a bed and breakfast.

The house was old and quaint and would be a great spot for it. We talked of all the wonderful people we would meet and have dinner with. The only thing that was needed was some more bedrooms and baths on the formal side of the house.

With the huge den, library and dinning room it would be a hit, I just knew it.

When mom and Bob pulled up for dinner the weather had gotten worse, there was no way they would be going home tonight, for sure. I had put mom's new mattress in my room for me to sleep on, my old twin was just too small for me and baby, and now with Jack in my bed it was a real need.

But I had bought a new sofa sleeper that was very soft to sleep on.

It had been on sale and I tough it would be great for company to sleep on.

When mother saw Jack she couldn't hold her approval back, she hugged and hugged us both over and over as tears rolled down her checks.

She saw the happiness that lit up both of our eyes when we looked at each other.

As both men went to fire up the fireplace mother and I hit the kitchen to finish up my dinner and talked. I told her everything that Jack had told me about his past and why he left. When I finished telling her there were tears in both of our eyes. I told her how much he loved the baby already and how he took hearing about my rape and impregnation by Jason.

We sat in the dinning room for hours eating drinking tea and talking about everything, including about making the farm into a bed and breakfast. Mother loved the ideal and decided she wanted to back it. We told her we would but she wouldn't hear of it, she had the money that the city hall paid her sitting in a bank doing nothing.

She loved how I had turned her room upstairs into a sitting room for us and it would give us space to have some privacy from the rest of the house.

We decided to have a architect draw up some plans that would add four bedrooms and baths.

We laughed and laughed for hours until mother saw my heavy eyelids and sent me to bed, she even rushed Jack to bed and her and Bob cleaned up the kitchen before they hit the hay too.

It was nice to spend time with mom and Bob, they fit tighter so well, it was hard not to believe that they had been together forever. I missed my dad very much but it was a great joy to see my mother happy and content.

It snowed all that day and night. When we woke the next morning it was still snowing hard, it snowed for three day's before letting up. The roads were so bad mother and

Bob stayed at the farm the rest of the week.

We watched movies, played spades and sit around the fireplace to keep warm. It was the most fun for us all four. Spending time learning new things about each other and bonding as a family.

Bingo spent all his time passed out in front of the fire. He would raise his head once in while to look around and pass out again. Bingo was six years old and starting to show his age, he had no need to go outside except to use the bathroom and he would hurry and run back inside to the fire.

Mother felt the baby move, she was so excited about having a grandbaby close. She only got to see James at holidays and most of the time it felt like strangers to us at first. We would spend most of the time they would visit getting to know each other all over again, each visit. I wanted my child to spend time with his or her grandmother and Bob, the only grandfather my child would have.

It was so nice to watch as Jack and Bob bonded, they got along so well. They kept the fire going and had wood stacked up. So it was nice and warm inside as we spend our days with each other.

I had gone shopping and we enjoyed making dinner for us all, one night the men even cooked for us ladies, surprising us with a great dinner of steak and salad with huge baked potatoes filled with sour cream and butter.

After a week the weather warmed up and the roads cleared. But before mom left we celebrated my birthday. it was February the second, ground hog day. Last year for my twenty-fifth I had not wanted to celebrate, with every thing that had happened but this year for my twenty-six I did.

This year I had everything I needed to be happy. A man who loved me and a child on the way.

We had a cake and took pictures for my baby's book. It was a truly wonderful day, that is until I answered the phone.

"Hello" I said very excited.

"Bitch. How can you be happy without daddy home? Miss me baby? I miss…" I screamed and dropped the phone. Jack came running in, saw the phone and picked it up.

"Who is this?" He asked furiously.

"Who's this asshole?" Was the answer on the phone.

"Jack. Who is this?" Jack answer back.

"I'm the baby's father, see my slut is up to her old ways. How is she treating you? You take care of her till I get home, ok."

"Like hell, now listen here this Jason, leave Cara-Ann and her baby alone, you understand, come near ether and your dead, you got that, dead, I'll see to it myself, you will never hurt her again. I'm going to raise the baby as mine, I'm going to marry Cara-Ann and we will be a family." I couldn't believe what I had heard Jack say to Jason, he was going to marry me.

“What the hell…” was all Jason got out as Jack hung up the phone.

“Guess I should have asked you first. But will you marry me Cara-Ann?” He asked as he fell on one knee in front of me.

“Yes, Yes, Yes.” Was all I could say.

Mother who was standing in the door watching screamed out loud.
“Yes a wedding.”

And we celebrated again.

Chapter 14
"The Homecoming"
By Deana Rae Higgins

Secret of the map

I had forgot about the map and the numbers on it, when out of the blue I said something to Jack and he asked if we had checked dad's safety deposit box at the bank.

"What box?" I turned to him and asked.

"The one your dad had at the bank at the bank over in Johnsonville."
Jack replied.

"Jack we had no knowledge of a box. Why didn't we find anything to tell us about it? I don't understand." I said softy as what Jack said sank in, a box. Wonder what we would find?

"He took me once when he went to put something in it, I

think it was a letter of some sort, but I'm not sure. I'm sorry I hadn't mentioned it to you before, I thought you surly found it by now."

I called mother right away, she had no knowledge of a box at the bank either, so we decided to go to town, mother gather up all the papers we would need, dad's death certificate and will, left Bob in charge of the drug store and hopped in Jacks truck with us.

The bank was located in Johnsonville which was about forty five minutes away, so what ever dad stashed in the box, he wanted to make sure it wasn't found by the wrong person.

The ride up was filled with tension, we couldn't come up with any reason for the cloak-and-dagger of the map or box, we decided, mother and I, that we didn't know dad at all, after all these years.

For him to hide so many secrets from mother was in a way unforgivable to her, any foolish remorse she felt for remarry, was wipe out that second.

We found the bank easy, as there was only two in Johnsonville; it was the first we tired.

We asked to speak to the manager and when we brought up dad's name, she turned her head sideways and said with a laugh.

"How funny, you're the second person to ask about this box holder, I received a call just this morning from someone asking if we had a box in this holder's name. That wasn't you who called, by chance?"

"Yes, it was. Can I see the box please? I have my papers here." mother stated, but we knew she hadn't called, or she would have mentioned it to us, someone in town picked up the party line when I called mother and told her, I knew better, it was my faugh, I had forgotten abut being careful.
With Jack around me I had become too trusting.

The lady from the bank talked all the way to the vault, about how sorry she was about mom's loss. She had met dad several times and he was a very sweet gentleman.

When we at last had privacy we opened the safety box. At the top was a letter to mother from dad, a second one, the one mother and I found hidden in there bedroom after his death talked of his love for her, nothing else. She tucked the letter away for now, to read later.

Next there was a letter for me and James, I tucked these away too. There were old, yellow, black and white pictures next, of dad's family, but we had never seen them before. The pictures was of a huge family, ten kids we counted, standing around a ranch, with there parents.
There were pictures of the same family in different phases of children born in all kinds of different places, like at the fair, in town.
We could see the town name in several pictures. In one picture, the one and only with all ten kids, there stands a small boy, who looked around two years old, who looked like the dad we knew. I looked at mother in confusion.

"Well now the pictures at home make sense." was all she said.

She sat the pictures down and again began to empty the box. There was a new will, which left everything to mother, James and me and the twins, equally. This was the same as the one we held, but with an added note.

"Any child of Cara-Ann's has the right to the family estate of my blood parents, the money is held at this bank in a trust for said child. Said money shall be divided among all children of Cara-Ann, the only blood relative of Jacob and June Harper, from me. If by change no children are born to Cara-Ann, all moneys will be given to blood sister's and brother's of Jacob and Jan Harper's, ten children. If none can be found, money shall go to James Raye Jr. All money will be held in a trust for said children of Cara-Ann until their twenty-first birthday. Cara-Ann will receive a sum of 0.01 percent of held trust, each month, for care of said child, and each child born to Cara-Ann will receive 0.01 percent of inheritance. Further more should Cara-Ann outlive all children born, all money's goes to Cara-Ann or her estate at her death." Mother read out loud, keeping her eyes down, when at last she finished, knowing full well I understood what dad meant, James wasn't dad's, mother would have a lot of explaining to do.

Under that were dad's birth record from the church in town and an adoption record of his adoption from the Raye's at the age of two, when his birth parents died in a freak accident from a company product that was huge at the time. There was a huge settlement and insurance on both parents. They both had been from old money.

There was old antique jewelry marked for me, from my grandparents and old bonds that looked very important to us. There were deeds to land in town we didn't know we owned but made sense when we discussed it later.

The same farms that dad would help out every year; he must have rented them to the family's cheap. And we never knew it and they, not once ever let it slip, when we would take over dinners and goods for the families. No wonder dad was so loved when he died.

Some of the land deeds had been made out to the family's that lived on the land that held the house, keeping the land around the homes in my name.

At last the box was empty except for a adoption record for James and dad's and mother's wedding license showing they married five months before James was born. Dad had legally adopted James to protect him and raise him as his own. Why he had to bring it out now, made me angry. I wished he had just kept that one secret.

Mother was very hurt by what dad's will had said, dad had promised never to tell anyone of her digression many years before.

I tried to help but I knew that this was one time that what she was feeling was her's alone to feel. My dad really let her down and I would never forgive him, he should and could have kept her secret.

"Let's go to the farm and talk." was the only thing mother said as we drove home.

My mind was going ninthly; I had asked about the inheritance at the bank before we left, the trust held two hundred and fifty six million dollars. Once my baby was born I would receive a check each month for twenty five thousand six hundred each month.

On one hand I was upset for mother and James when he found out the truth but on the other hand I was floored. How could dad had lived with this secret all his life and ours? How did he get everyone in town to go along with it?

And then it hit me and I made Jack pull over so I could throw up. Jason had known about the money, that's why he had to get me pregnant so he could try to get his hands on the money thru my baby.

The same thought must have hit both my mother and Jack for they looked at each other then at my belly then away. Now I really had to keep Jason away from me and my baby.

As I got back into the truck, Jack patted my back and told me not to worry, we would fix it. I knew he meant he would do what my dad had done and marry me and adopt my baby.

I was glad we had had the time before he left to get close, I would hate for him to make a commitment to me and the baby just to protect us. I had doubted Jack once I would never again.

We headed home without another word. When we arrived home mother called Bob and asked to come out, she needed to talk to all of us. James was too far to call home on short notice so we decided to wait to tell him. Mother said there was no way to tell this on the phone so she would ask James to come his next holiday off.

I heated some soup and mother made some ham and cheese sandwiches for us, I also made a pot of hot coffee, I felt we would need it.

When Bob arrived we all sat and talked as we ate. We only talked of light stuff for now, Bob never questioning my mother, knowing when she was ready she would spill, I was so glad mother had Bob, more then ever.

She would need him more then ever now and in the next weeks.

Slowly mother began to tell of our find at the bank, of the pictures and of the story behind the pictures. She told of the money and how dad was adopted, and then she told of James' adoption.

"I met your James Sr. or Jim as his friends called him, when I was young, we grew up together as friends. It wasn't until years later that we fell in love. Well at least for me your father said he loved me from the very second he saw me at church for the first time when we were five.

I used to laugh and tell him that was bologna but he would tell me, it was true.

We would study at each other home and spend all our free time together but only as friends. My senior year in high school I was dating Jims best friend at the time, a nice guy named Pete, Jim never dated, he was a poor farm boy and more into farming then dances and movies and dating.

One night the college over in Johnsonville had a party at the frat house for the guys who wanted to join. I went with Pete as his date, he was thinking about joining the frat. Pete was a rather smart boy who planned on going to college.

He got drunk one night and ran his car off the road at eighty five, rolling it three times and killing himself and his new girlfriend at the time, but I getting ahead of my self.

At the party they had a lot of liquor to drink, it was my

first time seeing all the parting that goes on in college and it really scared me. I had not known that Pete drank at any time much less as much as he did. When I found out he drank so much I dropped him, fast.

The trouble was I had, a cola to drink with no liquor in it, but somehow it got spiked and I passed out and so did Pete.

When I woke up the next morning my clothes had been removed and I had been raped, I had no ideal who or how many had raped me and I was not going to go thru that, trying to prove who it was. I can't image what James will think of me or himself.

When I told Jim. what had happened, well he got real mad, I didn't tell him right away, I waited until I found out I was pregnant. He went over to that frat house and destroyed it, when they put him in jail I got him out by not telling anyone what had happened to me that night. And until now I haven't, I am so angry that Jim made me tell, I never wanted James to know the truth, and now I have no choice.

I couldn't tell my folks about it so we told them that is was Jim's and we got married. After we married and James was born, Jim went to the county seat and adopted him too, so there would never be any say about who his father was or is, that's why I can't understand. Why now? So now you know the truth and why I got so mad that you didn't tell me Cara-Ann about what happened to you, I understand rape, far more then I want too.

Please lets never keep secrets again, ok."

"Oh mother, I'm so sorry, yes I'll never keep anything from you again, and I'll help you tell James if you want, I love you mother and you're the best mom ever I would never judge you and James won't either, you'll see." The words falling out of my mouth so fast, I was breathless afterwards and had to sit down. I held mothers hands as both Bob and Jack hugged mom and said the same things I had told her.

"Mother does that mean that the mayor is my uncle? I'm not calling him that or inviting him for Christmas!" I angrily stated a little too loud.

Everyone broke into laughter, loud releasing laughter that made me laugh too. And we felt better. Mother and Bob decided it was time to go home and hit the sack, it had been a long, exhausting day for both of them.

After they left Jack and I talked for hours, he wanted all the money that came in for the baby put in a account just for me and the baby. I told him I trusted him but he wanted it that way and that was that.

We set the date for our wedding, February the fourteen, Valentines Day. It was a romantic date for a perfect wedding.

And we set in motion the court papers to dissolve all rights to the baby from Jason and have Jack adopt the baby as his own.

We also talked about our dream of making the farm a bed and breakfast and we both wanted to go ahead with the dream, and the nice thing now, once the baby was born we would have more then enough money to help us with it.

We talked of how Jason must have known about the

whole thing, and wanted a part of the money.

We talked of the mayor and his buddies trying to take over our farm, maybe to make us leave town so we would not go after the money cause we wouldn't have known about it.

I could talk to my uncle but I wasn't going to except maybe to let him know, I know the secret of the map, my baby is the secret.

Chapter 15
"The Homecoming"
By Deana Rae Higgins

Mask of drama

I didn't have time to plan a huge affair for my wedding, but then I really didn't want one. A huge wedding that was.

We planed a small affair at the church, with Sam doing the honors. He wasn't happy at first about it, but he wasn't that unhappy either.

Everyone in town knew what Jason had done to me including the fact that I was carrying his child by force.

Sam seemed grateful I hadn't asked him to marry me and raise another mans child, course they had no knowledge of the money and I wondered if he would have changed his mind, had he known about it.

I picked a soft white dress, I would have worn mother's dress she wore when she married my dad, but after what he did to mother and James, I couldn't do it. We decided on a small dinner at the huge afterwards.

James couldn't come in for the wedding so we decided to wait to tell him what we had found out, the secret had waited this long it could wait longer.

Mother and Bob helped us out, if it had not been for their friends, we would have had no one there for the wedding.

We asked that instead of gifts to us they bring something for the church box for the needy.

So the guests went all out for the church, which was nice to see.

I knew that many would be help this year because of our wedding. It was a nice feeling. It was a really nice affair that went off without a hitch. I couldn't believe I was getting married.

I loved Jack so much and I knew that he loved and needed me as much as I did him.

We held hands and said our do's in front of Mom, Bob and most of the town as tears ran down many a face including mine and Jacks.

We all went to the farm and celebrated with good bar-be-que and a huge red and pink cake.

We had hung out lights around the front yard, and rented tables and chairs for the guests.

We cleaned out a spot for dancing and hired a band to play country songs as the town and us dance away the night.

I had bought a whole bunch of deposable cameras so everyone took pictures for us.
There were drinks for those who wanted and cold ice tea for those of us pregnant or who just didn't want to.

We danced and laughed and fun was had by all, it was a great day.

We didn't wrap up the party until midnight; boy was I tired when I fell into bed for my first night as a married woman.

"Cara-Ann Raye Atkins, Mrs. Jack Atkins, Mrs. Cara-Ann Atkins, Cara-Ann Atk…" Jack walked into the bedroom as I was trying out my new name.

"Mrs. Atkins. So are you happy babe? Laughing out loud at me.

"I am Mr. Atkins. Come here and I'll show you how much." I purred.

"Why Mrs. Atkins, I'm a married man. Or you trying to seduce me?"

"Kiss me and I tell you." And he did over and over that night and I told him many times how much I loved him.

As we made love that night we became closer then I ever though possible.

After we made love for what seemed like hours we held each other as we drifted to sleep in each others arms, so in love with each other and feeling like best friends as well, I drifted to sleep dreaming of us together till death do us part.

I saw the farm big and beautiful again and full of life. I saw many kids in our future not just the one I carried. There was a Jack Jr. and a couple of girls running around.

We had horses and a huge garden that the girls help me keep clean of weeds.

I saw my men fishing and bringing home big fish for me to fry. It was a wonderful dream and I knew I had made the right choice in trusting Jack again.

Morning found me well rested and happy. When I woke Jack was downstairs fixing breakfast for me, I had truly found a good man, and I could smell the bacon cooking and suddenly I felt pangs of hunger.

We sat, talked about how nice the day before was, visited with Bingo, and read the paper like any other couple. Our first day as man and wife started off great.

We called several builders for quotes for the bedrooms we wanted to put in.

We decided to go with an older wooden look like a cabin in the woods.

We also wanted to put in a fishing lake for our guests to use.

I wanted horses for myself and guests to use, and at first Jack argued with me but it was in fun, I knew he wanted horses too.

We spend the day dreaming and everything was going great until we got visitors that let us unhappy.

We were having coffee and sandwiches on the porch when they drove in from behind the farm, so we didn't see them until they pulled up in a pile of dust in a big truck. Four big guys. Jason's brothers. They jumped out and started walking to the door.

"Stop, that's close enough. What can I do for you gentlemen?" Jack asked.

"Their Jason's brothers." I whispered softly.

"No worry's babe." Jack whispered back winking at me.

"WE want to talk about Jason's kid! He deserves to know how its doing. Your not going to keep this baby from him you know, and soon as his lawyer proves you wasn't raped he'll be free." Spitting on the grass, leaving a dark brown spot, when he finished talking.

"Well I got a message for your brother, you tell him that my wife and baby are none of his concern and if I ever see you boys around here any more, I'm going to shoot first then asked why after, understand." Jack said very calmly.

"What the hell you say, well he isn't going to like it, no sir, he won't."

"I don't care what he likes or doesn't like, this is my home, my wife, my child, and if anyone try's to hurt them, they going to have to answer to me, got it." Jack yelled back, standing now."

“Well mister, that’s not how its going to be see my brother is that baby’s father and he has his reason for holding on to…” The oldest brother said as he walked closer to the screen door.

“Yea the money. Huh?” I snapped before I realized what I had said.

“You know about the money, that money is rightfully my brothers too as that baby’s daddy, sides that not your money that’s the mayor’s family’s money and you should just do the right thing Cara-Ann and give it back.”

“Cara-Ann get my gun, I think its time these men got off our land.” Jack stated.

“In fact this here dog has been wanting to bite someone, so if you don’t get in your truck and get the hell off my land I will turn him lose on you, now.” As Jack talked he walked over to the screen with Bingo right on his heels, Bingo wanted out. When they saw that Jack meant business they got in the truck and started it up.

“We will be back you fools, you’ll see, we will give your best to Jason Cara-Ann, you will be hearing from us again. You can bet on that, for sure.” And with that they took off as fast as they came in, in a whirl of dust.

As they left I ran to Jack and flung myself into his arms as tears flowed down my cheeks, I was so proud of the way he had handled them and the way he stood up for me and the baby.

"Its ok baby, I protect you and the baby, I love you both, you my life."

And I knew that I was and he would.

We called the sheriff's and made a report but they didn't really do anything wrong. Yet.

I knew and Jack knew they wouldn't give up; it was worth it to them to keep it up. There was a lot of money involved here and they wanted a share of it, bad, no matter what they had to do to get it.

Over the next week, nothing out of the ordinary happened. Jack and I spent time with each other.

We spent time looking over the plans for the new addition of the house, it was fun to pick out colors and designs. We decided to go with a late 1800's look, dark velvets, cherry woods, white lace and home made quilts on the beds.

One day as we sat in our kitchen drinking coffee and talking, we heard Bingo start barking from his fenced yard out front. We had put up a small fenced pen for him to lay outside in the sun. jack got up to look out the window as the blacks brothers drove by with one driving and one in the back with a gun, pointed at the house, at Bingo.

"No! You assholes, oh my god, no."

I watched as Jacks face went from mad to horror as they shot and killed Bingo. Jacks face went snow white as he watched from the window, he ran out side too late to stop the Black brothers or to save Bingo. Bingo died instantly from the bullet going thru his heart. I was grateful Bingo hadn't suffered; we buried him under the huge oat tree out front, his favorite space to lay and watch the squirrels and birds.

They wanted war, we wanted peace and our Bingo paid with his life.

Chapter 16
"The Homecoming"
By Deana Rae Higgins

Tammy and Tanner

I couldn't believe that Bingo was gone. He had been my best friend. As I went thru the next few days I would forget and call him before I remembered he was dead.

Jack found me one day out by this grave, crying my eyes out. When I tried to get up I felt weak and almost passed out, it scared Jack so bad he called the doctor out on a house call.

Jack went to the sheriff to see if anything could be done but with no evidence to prove who did it there was nothing to go on.

The doctor said complete bed rest for me so I went to bed and read and slept. I caught up on reading every magazine I could find. Caught up on the mail and found a wedding invite for Tammy and Tanner.

They decided to get married, how sweet, I decided to talk to mother about giving them an acre of land that stood on the far side of ours, it had lots of trees for shade, and they could build a house for themselves and their children. I understood completely why Tanner and I drifted apart. I had really like him a lot and I wanted to something nice for them both.

I called mother and she agreed it was a wonderful ideal for a gift.

Dad would have approved a lot. We picked out a nice acre with road access. It had trees and beautiful green grass. It would make a fine home for them to start a family.

Perhaps my child will have a play mate. It was the middle of March and I was seven months into my pregnancy.

It seemed like forever ago that Jason raped me. I had recovered to a better woman. I would be the best mom I could be and Jack the best dad, I just knew it.

We were happy and I, we wanted the whole world to feel the same way.

On Sunday's mom and Bob would come over for dinner after church. It was the best day of the week for me.

My mother had never looked so happy and in love, the smile on her face warmed my heart.

We would call James and talk for hours to him, his wife Kelly and the twins.

It was a happy time, it was spring, and the birds were chirping, the sun shinning bright and flowers blooming galore.

Jack was very busy with the farm, so I spent time alone, preparing for my baby.

I learned to quilt and knit, watched a lot of television and read every thing I could find with print in or on it.

I would clean the house, careful not to over do it, cook something for supper and wait for Jack.

He would come home at dark, tired and dirty. I would feed him, send him to bath while I cleaned up the kitchen and join him in bed. It wouldn't take long for both of us to fall asleep from exhaustion.

We would talk just enough to keep up on the news of our day and fall asleep in each others arms, held there by love.

One night in late March, I was dreaming of Jason and his brothers. They broke into our home as we slept.

I could hear the loud roar of the truck that Jason's

brothers drove, it was so loud, and it sounded like it was in the house.

Jack and I awoke at the same time, the noise was real, and it was outside our front door. Jack ran downstairs while I called the sheriff, I begged him to wait, but he wouldn't.

The loudness of the truck's motor got louder, as it was revved up. I could hear jack yelling as he got to the door.

Then a horrible noise as the truck hit the porch, ramming into the front door.

My blood turned cold as the house shook and my mind though of Jack.

"Jack!" I yelled his name and tried to go down the back stairs but was cut off halfway by debris in my way.

I heard the motor start up again, it had died out on impact, I ran up and away from the front stairs as the truck ripped out of the hole it made in the kitchen, pulling the back stairs down and apart as the truck descended from the house.

I could hear the damage as I ran to the front stairs, yelling for Jack the whole time.

As I reached the bottom of the stairs I knew it was bad, I could see the whole back of the house was destroyed, I couldn't see Jack nor could I hear him.

I was standing in the middle of the front stairway

breezeway when the police showed up.

I yelled that Jack was in the kitchen and that a truck hit the house. I allowed myself to be led out to the arriving ambulance to check on my baby, I had fallen upstairs when the house shook from the truck leaving the house.

It took a while for the police and firemen to clear a pate into the kitchen without doing more damage to the house and making the roof fall on top of their heads and Jacks.

They found him in the bathroom behind the kitchen. He has a huge lump on his head from being thrown into the wall when the truck hit, he had seen the headlights moving as he stopped at the bottom of the stairs and ran away into the bathroom door as the truck hit the back porch, plowing thru the door into the kitchen stopping halfway thru the back stairs.

If the truck had went more right into the front of the house Jack would surly have been hurt or killed.

When I saw them bring Jack out walking on his own two feet, I started to cry and tried to move to run to him but couldn't as I was hit with a very hard pain followed by a huge gush of liquid. I yelled out in pain as a second hard deep pain hit my stomach, the baby was coming. Early.

"Hurry Jack, we got a baby coming, fast." They yelled for Jack to run and as his feet hit the back bumper board of the ambulance they shut the doors and sped away with Jack and me inside.

I prayed for my baby's safety. It was six weeks early and was coming out, no if and or buts. I felt Jack beside me as we raced for the hospital in town; his hand found mine and held on, praying with me. I had never seen Jack pray before, and I realized how much he loved me and our baby.

I screamed as pain three hit with such force I dug my nails into Jacks hand, making him scream out in pain too. He didn't try to pull away or scold me. He allowed me to hold his hand freely, taking the pain I dished out, with joy and encouragement to me.

He told me later he felt very connected to me and the baby at the time and it bonded us forever, all three of us. By the time we arrived at the hospital I no longer could count the contraction's as they had become one long contraction. We arrived just as the baby's head crowned, I could feel the tearing of my soft skin as the baby's head pushed forward, pushing my legs apart.

They moved me into a room just as the baby's shoulder's appeared. Jack looked at the beautiful blond head and moved beside the doctor to make sure his child was not dropped. He didn't let go of my hand, forcing me to sit up and pushing the baby out and I screamed in pain, closing my eyes shut at the pain.

Jack watched as his daughter came in to the world, not missing any part. He said he had watched many a birth on the farm but none as wonderful as the birth of his daughter, not even when his favorite horse was born.

'

"I love you Cara-Ann, Thank you."
This made me laugh as I looked at my daughter, so perfect. And proud as I looked at my husband. The baby was so small, only five pounds and two ounces at birth, but crying healthy and loud.

She had reddish blond hair and big blue eyes, and looked like my dad. I hoped she would keep dad's blue eyes and red blond hair, I would teach her about her grandfather, that made her a rich little girl.

The nurse's took her to be weighed and measured. I turned to look at Jack; he was smiling from ear to ear.

Suddenly the monitor that was on my heart started going fast, sounding off a alarm, I watched as Jack's smile turned to fear and what looked a scream, I couldn't hear anything but the sound of the alarm as I drifted backwards in my eyes and my hearing, as if my bed had been shoved hard back into the wall, only the bed wasn't moving, I was, but I wasn't.

I reached for Jack as a soft white could covered me, blocking off everything around me, all sound, all sight gone, replaced with a stillness.

All around me was huge green trees, soft green grass and fields of flowers, the smell was intoxicating. I was standing beside a huge tree, touching it with my left hand, grounding myself. I looked ahead and saw a blue lake, the light shinning on it, sparkling like a diamond filled lake. It held my glaze, pinning my eyes to the sparkle.

Across the lake I could see the source of the bright light, like a huge round white sun lying on the water top, moving closer as I watched.

The light consuming everything around into the light so that all that could be seen was the light. I stood watching the light, with my hand flat against the tree, somehow knowing that if I let go all traces of my life would be forgotten.

I could feel the love and peace that filled the white light, feeding it as it moved closer and closer to me. The closer the light moved to me, I began to see people standing in the light, with a man in front of the line.

Every where I looked from side to side stood shadow's of people, men, woman, and children, laughing and reaching for me. The closer they got the more I saw loved ones that I had lost in death, I recognized the man in front as Jesus, beside him stood my dad. Jesus reached for me with both arms open wide; I had never felt such love and brightness.

The warmth ness of the light radiated in front of the light, making the end of my fingers as I reached out my free right hand. I was going to let go of the tree and step forward when from behind me I heard my name called, I barely heard it, when I heard it called again, this time louder.

I knew the voice that called my name it was Jack. I looked at my father and other family members before me. I looked at Jesus and felt at peace.

The love around him was the strongest I had ever felt, I would forever be changed by it. The light that lifted his feet off the grown drifted like smoke, moving him forward.

Again I heard my name and remembered my life, my child my husband, my mother, all things I loved on earth, and with a hesitations I turned and let go of the tree walking back to the voice of my husband calling my name, the name giving to me by my mother.

I awoke to Jack beside me screaming my name. I reached out my hand and patted his chest, whispering softly, its ok, I'm back, and I'm not going any where. Jack laid his head against my chest and cried, hugging me declaring his love for me and devotion forever. I made a mental note to never forget what I had felt and seen, I knew the answer to life I knew the truth about god and death, and I would enjoy both, but life first.

Jack wouldn't leave my side as they moved me into my room. He fluffed my pillow, tucked me in, ordered some food and drink for me, barking at the nurse's. they just patted my arm and said its ok, its very normal.

We looked at each other, seeing only each other in a room full of strangers, as we each though of the same thing. What to name our new daughter? I laughed at Jack fussing over me so much and sent him to call my mother, and find our daughter.

Ten minutes later Jack came back into my room. I had freshened up some and changed into a hospital gown as my bag didn't make it past the back door.

Jack walked over to me with a dozen red roses in hand and set the vase on the nightstand, leaned in and kissed me just as the nurse rolled the basinet into the room, leaving our daughter; she turned and left the room shutting the door on her way out.

Jack picked her up ever so gentle and laid her in my arms.

She was awake and alert. She was very small and very pale. She looked like a doll from my childhood. And I knew her name.

“Annabelle Jean Johnson, welcome to your family.” I whispered softly.

“Annabelle Jean. I like that, after my mom, Jean, how sweet. Yep I like it. How about you Annabelle, like it? Shall we call you Belle for short?”

And as in answer, Belle moaned and closed her eyes to rest, she had a hard day coming into this world, it was March 28, Belle’s birthday.

Chapter 17
"The Homecoming"
By Deana Rae Higgins

And baby makes three

Mother came to the hospital with Bob. As mother held her new granddaughter Belle, Jack explained what had happened, including the part I hadn't heard.

When the Black brother's crashed into our porch they left behind a part of their truck when they left, the front license plate.

And before they could get rid of the truck the brothers where caught, driving the truck, both where very intoxicated. Both taken to jail, to pay for there crimes.

The payment, loss of their freedom.

While mother stayed with me and Belle at the hospital, Bob and Jack saw to the remodeling of our kitchen and back door.

They decided to put in glass sliding doors that allowed the light to fill the kitchen. They also widened up the laundry room and put in bigger stairway with lots of light, no more dark small stairway.

Sense the Black boys took out most of the kitchen we also got new appliance's, new modern ones. And with the bed and breakfast coming along, Jack put in two ovens and a huge stove top.

They expanded the porch into a garden area with huge windows on three sides. With soft padded chairs and small tables for sitting around drinking coffee or what ever the mood wanted.

They hung pots of hanging flowers that smelled of heaven all around. And put in a pot belly fireplace for the winter months.

It would become mine and Belle's favorite place.

We would spend hours watching daddy work on the farm. The kitchen looked like a whole different kitchen and cooking in there was a joy. With the new dishwasher and refrigerator that had ice and water in the door, I felt spoiled.

The trial for the Black boys was hard for me; sense they knew I had the baby. I knew that when Jason found out he would try to make trouble for us. They both got sentenced for thirty five years each and would be joining their big brother in jail.

On the way out of the court room, they both made sure I understood that they would be giving Jason a full report on the birth of my daughter.

Jack held me as they ranted and raved as they were escorted out of the court room by the sheriff's, it helped but still the hair on the back of my neck told me it wasn't over yet.

"You will get yours Cara-Ann, wait until Jason hears he has a daughter just wait!"

It took six weeks to finish the repairs to the house, so Belle and I stayed in town with mother and Bob.

Jack stayed at the farm and saw to the men working, but he would come to town for dinner every night to see us.

The light that filled his eyes every time he saw Belle filled my eyes with tears. He would hold her and talk to her with a sweetness I knew he held inside.

We would sit for the longest time, him holding Belle and I curled up next to him. Belle would wake every night to the sound of his sweet voice and lay there looking in to his eyes and mine as if she understood every word he said to her and then fall back asleep curled up in Jacks arms.

Every night he would tenderly kiss me goodbye and tell me it was killing him not to be with his wife and daughter.

When he left, I would stand there tears rolling down my face until I couldn't see the tail lights on his truck.

It was the first of May when we moved back home, it was so wonderful and new, it was like a new house yet the same old comfortable home we knew and loved.

It was hot already, but Jack had updated the air and heat when he redid the kitchen and the new porch area had cool air. Belle and I stayed in there during the day watching the men plowing the fields and working the land. I really enjoyed watching the land become green with plants laid in nice neat rows.

Mother would come by to sit and watch the transformation, it had been so long sense the land was planted with crops that I swear I saw tears on her face but she denied it, of course.

The farm was alive and growing bigger and better every day.

After tea and gossip mother would send me to take a nap and she and her granddaughter would spend time in the new porch area watching the land bloom.

I would wake to wonderful smells coming from the new kitchen, mother enjoyed cooking, but to get to use

her old but new kitchen made it even more enjoyable.
She would cook enough to take to Bob and leave us to enjoy our home cooked meal by our self's.

One night I dreamed that daddy came to see me, he was so happy about the farm and all the wonderful things that Jack and I had done to the farm.

He was very happy over his new granddaughter, Belle and kept ringing a bell in his right hand, I couldn't understand it, but in the dream it was funny.

A few nights later, I was awoken by the door bell ringing, over and over. I woke Jack and sent him down stairs to check, thou he said he hadn't heard anything. While he left, I rose to check on Belle and got the scare of my life, the cover somehow was coving her face and she looked a soft blue tint, I grabbed her and blew air into her face and the color blue turned to a soft pink

When Jack returned he said no one was at the door, which didn't surprise me, I knew it had been my dad warning me about the blanket covering Belle's face. I moved Belle bed closer to ours and thanked my dad for warning me, I could fell his sprit all around me, protecting me and Belle from harm, and it comforted me.

I would wake to foot steps in the hall and I would recognize them as my dad's, he would walk the hall when I was young to check on me and James and the homestead. So it didn't surprise me that he still did it. Jack just laughed when I told him, calling me a tried woman. But mother agreed with me that daddy's ghost could be living in the house that he loved more then life itself.

Summer raged on with heat and fire dry days that drained the life out of the land. The crops where harvested and sold. The neighbors cupboards filled to the top told of our good fortune.

The inn was done and we planned the opening for October.

We decorated for Halloween, bringing bails of hay up front for a nice spot to tell scary stories. We had six rooms we could rent and once we caught on they were filled every weekend and sometimes during the week.

We would have dinner in the huge dinning area, all of us sitting around the table. Mother and Bob would join us a lot; mother would help with the cooking and cleaning.

But I felt she would come just to talk with our guests who would sit at our table for dinner.

Several times I would find mother standing in a old part of the farm, white as a ghost, I always knew the reason, she would see my dad standing in different parts of the farm watching her.

At first it scared her thinking my father would be mad she remarried but once she saw him watching Bob and smiling she knew he wasn't mad, but happy.

We accepted the fact that we had a haunted house, and at first only mother or I would see or hear them but as time went on, we knew we had more then one ghost and the guests saw them and heard them many times.

Our bed and breakfast became very popular with ghosts hunters.

We had named the farm, "Times past" on the internet when we posted our ad for the bed and breakfast. With the ghosts joining our home, it fit so we hung a sign out front naming the farm.

People from our town and towns close to us would come to stay at our farm to "Ghost spy". It seemed like the more strangers that stayed with us the more ghosts we had. Some would call us liars and thief's, saying it was fake, but those who knew the truth, would always see, hear or feel something to make them happy and scared.

A lot of times, I would find Belle in her bed looking at someone or something only she could see, laughing and smiling. Small children can see what we as adults can no longer see. The peter pan syndrome. Adults grow up and don't believe so their for they stop seeing or hearing what there mind will not accept.

The inn became a huge hit and we found ourselves very busy all the time, we even hired help from town to help with all the chores.

Belle loved having other kids that would come stay with there parents in the house.

James and his family came in for the holidays, we saved a spot for then to stay with us, the twins had a room and James and his wife a room. The twins loved Belle as she did them, I would find one of them carrying Belle around all day long, she got so spoiled by them she cried when they left to go back home.

They had planned James' vacation to take with us for the holidays. It was the New Year before they left and we all missed them, we all tried hard to talk them into moving back home but all we got was, we'll think about it.

With my inheritance checks coming in no one needed money, but James was more upset over finding out that he wasn't dad's, that he left with a chip on his shoulder and wanted nothing to do with my money from dad.

It was hard to tell James about it and we tried very hard to make him understand it changed nothing in our hearts.

It was January and Belle was crawling all over the

place. She would be turning one soon, she was a very bright child.

Jack was very protective of her, making sure everything in the house was child safe. She had her seat right next to his at the head of the table with my chair on the other side, she was his world, and I could see it and it made me very proud of my husband. We received several prank phone calls during this time but Jack took care of it and I relaxed.

Before we knew it, it was planting time again and Belle's birthday.

We had been so busy that we had forgotten our own birthdays, but not Belle's.

We had a huge party at the farm and even James, Kelly and the twins came in for a few days.

The twins had turned seven, and Lacy and Stacy looked just like their mother with her blue eyes.

I could tell that Kelly had been working on James about moving home, she wanted to move here with the girls so they could be close to us. Kelly's family was gone and her brother never talked to her so the only family she had was us.

James seemed a litter better about finding out the truth about dad but he still had some anger issues that he needed to deal with first.

The haunting' of the inn had gotten so bad that some nights it was hard to sleep with the noise from the guests and ghosts. The guests would stay up waiting to spy a ghosts and film it.

James and Jack would laugh there buts off where ever a guest would tell of there haunting story at dinner.

Belle would look from both of them, and laugh with them not knowing why, just that something was funny, the rest of the guests would laugh with Belle, just to laugh with her.

It became a regular thing, to laugh our way thru dinner enjoying the company of family and new friends.

Our life was happy and prosperous, filled with love and laughter, we would need these memories to help us thru the times that soon would befall us in the day's ahead. Trouble was coming our way in the form of the devil himself, using the name of Jason and his brothers. The Black boys had a score to settle with us, leaving death in their path.

Chapter 18
"The Homecoming"
By Deana Rae Higgins

Trouble comes for us

Mother was watching Belle for us at the farm when the call came in, it scared her so much she called Bob at work and had him close early to come and sit with her.

Jack and I had gone on an over night trip to look at some furniture we wanted to pick up for the rooms to give it a more antique look.

When we arrived home both mother and Bob were very upset, it seemed that the Black brothers had escaped from prison. They had killed a guard on the way out so the whole state was looking for him, but this didn't help us feel better.

We sent mom and Bob home to pack some things so that they could stay with us at the farm, just until the Black boys had been caught and returned to prison.

We called up the best body guard company that we could find close and hired two men with guns and dogs to cover the farm and us.

We even canceled the reservations for the next week so that we could have the farm to ourselves.

And then we waited for the Blacks or news they had been caught.

We were ready for them inside and out and just in case I found dad's old shotgun and his buck shot and loaded it, tucking it under my bed for safe and easy access.

We had been working so hard on the farm and in the inn that a small vacation from the inn work felt good, we couldn't shy from the farm work but we had help with that. So we canceled next week's guest and decided we needed the time off.

We also used the time to paint and update the rooms with the antique furniture that we found.

It took four days before a report came in that the Blacks had been sighted coming in our direction.

Belle was talking and walking by this time and

very much a daddy's baby. She would still take a nap during the day and with the men outside we felt safe, we were wrong.

Somehow they got past the guards by hitting them with drugged darts, and up stairs into Belle's room, which used to be my parents room but was Belle's now, and was gone with her before we knew what had happened. We never heard a sound; they had taken down the guards and dogs without making any noise.
I remembered that the Blacks would hunt the same way for deer or what ever else they felt like having for dinner, including your chickens, pigs or cows, all without a sound to alert you to what was going on.

I had warned everyone that the Black brothers could be very tricky but they hadn't taken me serious. Now they did, and my daughter was paying the price. I knew Jason wouldn't hurt his daughter, or at least I hoped he wouldn't.
They looked at his parent's home for the boy's but they had packed and left town rather suddenly. No one knew where they had gone in a hurry, but I knew they had gone with Jason so his mom could help with the care of a baby, her grandchild.

I yelled, I screamed, I cussed and then I cried, my baby was with a madman, the devil himself and she was in danger, I could feel it.

Jack was so angry at himself for not protecting

Belle; he had trusted the guards way too much and had put the running of the farm a head of us. I saw his pain and added to it blaming him for Belle disappearance too. I knew I shouldn't but my pain was so huge that I could only feel my own or really care about my own.

My baby was gone and I felt that I had been killed and left to walk the world as the walking dead. All I felt was pain and loss. My arms ached to feel my baby in them. I hated Jason with a hatred that I knew would allow me to kill him myself given the chance.

I prayed for my baby to be return home soon and shut Jack out, desperate to blame him.

Jack spent every waking hour working with the authorities on finding the Black family.

The news had their pictures posted at every post office in every state.

They put her picture and the Black brother's pictures on the news and on 'America's Most Wanted'. There was no way that sooner or later they would be seen and caught.

I cried all day and all night, when I wasn't sleeping from the drugs that the doctor gave me to sleep.

Jack spent his days helping answer phones and tracing down leads, he wouldn't even come home to sleep, which was fine with me, as I really didn't want to see him, I blamed him so much for my daughter's disappearance.

Mother stayed at the farm with me, leaving Bob in town alone. I begged her to go home that I would be fine but she wouldn't hear of it, for now.

There were reports coming in from all over, but there were some that seemed to have a pattern to them, like they were going in circles around us, me, the farm. When Jack saw this, he came home and sent mother home, this time he would be ready for them.

They were coming for me, Belle's mother and the one person in charge of the money.

Jack made some calls to a few friends who came to stay with us, some men he had know in his past. They set up a post with cameras and television's around the whole farm; they put everything in the outer room upstairs and could see every part of the farm from that one bedroom.

And then we waited and waited some more. The boys played cards and told old 'war' stories from back in the days. I went into Belle's room and slept on her couch for hours on end, waking only to go to the bathroom. I lost thirty pounds during this time, my clothes hung on me but Jack would barely look at me, any time we ran across each other, if he noticed he said nothing.

February came and my birthday without any

celebration, Jack didn't even remember at all.

I was up and moving around the house more but I still cried and prayed my way thru my days and nights.

I washed and cleaned my way to a tiredness that helped me sleep with out help from the drugs the doctor had given me.

The farm had never been cleaner.

The calls still came in about sightings, they moved in a wide circle then a small circle around us, changing up the route to lose the cops tracking them down. We even hired private investigators to track them. But the calls suddenly stopped and the trail went cold.

The call came in while I was alone in the kitchen and with out thinking I answered it. It was Jason mother, she was scared and worried, the baby seemed to be sick and she needed her mother, me.

I was told to leave without telling anyone where I was going and to drive south, I did just that too.

I slipped out and was gone in the truck before they could stop me, in the rearview I could see Jack run after me, I went west first to throw Jack off then turned south and drove. I had flattened the tires on his friend's car so there was no way for Jack or his friends to follow me. And if they called in help they would look west of town for me.

I drove for forty-five minutes before out of no where there was a truck behind me fast. They pulled in front of me and stopped making me slam on my brakes, then Jason pulled me out and his brother jumped in and drove off in my truck as Jason pulled me to his truck and shoved me in the back seat and took off, telling me to stay down.

I did as I was told and stayed down; we drove for an hour then pulled on to a gravel road for around thirty minutes before stopping. I got out and looked around, it was dark and all I could hear was the sounds of country woods. Suddenly I heard Belle crying and ran to the cabin and the sound of my baby.

I almost tripped in the dark but Jason was right beside me and grabbed me to help me, I cringed at his touch and he laughed at me.

"Ah baby, just wait and see what I have in store for us!" He spat at me.

Belle was lying on the only bed in the cabin, no one was holding her or talking to her, in fact at first I couldn't see anyone around but Belle.

"How could leave her alone?" I screamed as I picked her up. She knew me at once and hugged me crying harder.

“Bad mama.” she would say in between sobs. I held her, rocking her in my arms and cried with her.

I felt so relieved that my child was safe and in my arms again, I didn’t even care that now both of us was being held hostage by the Black brothers.

The youngest came out of the bathroom and I knew he had been left to watch Belle, where the parents where, I had no knowledge but must have tired of running and stopped and settled in somewhere to hide from the news showing there faces to the world.

I looked at Belle and she looked fine except she too had lost weight and looked tired, after we both cried for the longest time we feel asleep on the bed in each other’s arms. Belle had her arms wrapped around my neck and wouldn’t let go, I too held her to my chest and I didn’t want to let go, I would protect my baby to the death.

We slept until morning holding each other all night. I awoke to sweet kisses from Belle and her sweet voice calling me.

“Mama wake, mama wake.” She said over and over. Her sweet smile was all I needed to see.

I raised my head and saw Jason asleep in a chair with his feet on the bed, when he heard Belle laughing at me he awoke and looked at me. Fear shot thru me making my stomach jump and turn.

"Boo!" Jason screamed when he saw my fear, making me and Belle jump, making Belle start to cry.

"Damn sissy bitch, just like you, guess daddy will have to make her meaner." Jason spit out.

"You stay away from my daughter, you hear me." I scream out loud, making Jason jump to his feet grabbing Belle out of my arms and laughing at me. I jumped up and ran after him as he ran around with Belle in his hands, crying and reaching for me he stopped and I caught him grabbing Belle and hugging her tight.

"Feed her." was all he said as he opened the outside door and went outside, shutting the door behind him.

I looked around the small and dirty cabin, there were no windows and only one door in and out, and the one Jason went out. There was no phone and no television. Just an old refrigerator, bed and the chair that Jason slept in. I wonderer where the brothers had gone when suddenly I heard them outside. They walked in carrying groceries from the local store. Brave fools I thought. I prayed that they had been seen.

Belle and I ate and ate; we made up for lost time. The boys had picked up every news paper and magazine with there pictures on them to read.

They also had picked up an old couch that had seen its better days and an old black and white television. They looked as if they planned to stay put here for a while, which could be a good thing, sooner or later one of them would be recognized by someone.

It was late summer and hot, there was no air conditioner and with no windows no fresh air to cool us off. They had picked up an old fan that helped move the stale air around. Belle and I slept and ate in the long hot days.

It had been three weeks sense I had come to Belle, Jason seemed to be on his best behavior because of his brothers. He would lie beside me and Belle at night. To watch us and make sure we didn't try to run. What he didn't understand was I wanted to run but I couldn't take my daughter out in to what ever there was outside and keep her safe from harm, there was no telling where we were or how far from anyone else. And it looked deep in the woods to me and not a very safe place for a small child to be. So I stayed and waited.

Almost a month into my capture, my way out came to me. When the boys went to town to get beer and cigarettes they where recognized by the woman who ran the liquor store. She was a big fan of 'America's Most Wanted' and every Saturday night sense Belle had been kidnapped they showed the pictures and ran the story.

Belle and I were sleeping on the bed with Jason on the side facing the door when there was a huge sound of gun fire outside.

Belle and I rolled over on the floor and under the bed. Jason and his brothers jumped up and started firing gun fire back out side thru the walls of the cabin. They continued to fire their guns off making swiss cheese of the front cabin wall until all there ammo had been used.

Then the front door was pushed in from the outside, coming apart in pieces of wood. There was more gunfire inside the house and loud shouting.

"Cara-Ann, where are you? Stay down. Stop firing your guns, my wife and baby is in here. Cara-Ann" I heard Jack shout above the gun fire and then silence.

Belle was screaming at the top of her lungs so it was easy for Jack to find us, he lifted the bed up and shoved it over, picking me and Belle up in to his arms in one quick movement. Belle knew her daddy at once and grabbed him and swarmed on to his chest.

The only light was coming in from outside from the headlights of the horde of police cars that answered to call. I could see that the brothers had done well in the fight, and as I walked pass Jason, I saw he was dead, shot in the head and chest.

As I looked around it appeared as if all three brothers where killed in the fight and I sighed a sigh of relieve. The Blacks would not be a menace to us, any more.

"The parents, where they found?" But Jack shook his head no, there was no sign of them, yet he added.

As we got into the back seat of Jacks friends car, the three of us held each other and cried.

"I'm so sorry my girls, I let you down, it will never happen again." Jack whispered between his sobs.

"I'm sorry Jack for blam…" Jack cut me off with a soft kiss.

"Dadda, dadda, dadda, me kiss." Belle yelled as she pulled herself between us and wrapped a arm around us both. We both laughed and leaned in to kiss her on each side of her checks.

"More kiss, more kiss." Belle laughed holding us tight. We stayed that way for the trip home, kissing and laughing the whole way.

Chapter 19
"The Homecoming"
By Deana Rae Higgins

Home sweet home

Mother was sitting at the kitchen table when I came in the back door. She had come over to make sure that the farm was clean and made dinner for us. She jumped up and ran over to me grabbing both me and Belle.

Mother then grabbed Jack and hugged him.

"I knew you would bring them both home Jack, I just knew it. I'm so proud of you, thank you for bring my babies home."

I decided a bath for both me and Belle was in order,

and clean clothes. So I left Jack to tell mother about every thing that happened.

Best thing I ever did was to marry Jack and make him Belles dad. He loved the two of us more then he loved his own life, I knew that when I heard him put his life in danger to save the two of us.

I prayed that with the Blacks brothers dead our life would be peaceful and safe, but I also knew that the mom, dad and littlest Black brother had got away, and would be a threat to us until they all had been caught. I had the one thing they still wanted more then anything, their grandbaby.

I put Belle to bed, she was so tired she could hardly keep her eyes open, when I laid her in her bed, in her bedroom; she smiled and went to sleep.

Mother stayed the night in Belles room sleeping on the couch, I told she didn't need to but she wouldn't hear of it.

"I'll feel better and so will you, just for the night, that way you and Jack don't have to worry about her. Grandma will stay and watch over her tonight, she has been gone too long for me and I need some time to be close to her."

And with that she left Jack and me down stairs alone for the fist time in so very long, and neither of us was mad at each other.

Jack and I spent time talking before we went upstairs to bed make up for lost time. It had been along time that we had been close as a married couple and it felt good to touch each other and kiss. We took our time to enjoy each other knowing we could sleep as late as we wanted the next morning.

We awoke late to the sound of rain. It rained off and on for the next few weeks. It was early spring and it would be a green one this year. The grass, the trees, the crops in the field, all green and laden with fruit and vegetables.

It would be a wonderful planting season this year and our neighbors would be blessed for the winter months ahead with shelves full of our harvest.

Before we knew it, it was April and Belle was turning two. We decided that it was to be a big affair with all our friends, family and neighbors coming, a celebration of life, love and freedom.

We sent out the word for James, Kelly and the girls to come in for a visit, to our surprise they said yes without having to be begged. And they arrived we found out why.

"Pregnant with a baby, a boy! And we're moving back home, here. If you'll have us?" James and Kelly said together in unison.

"Of course, we would love to have you move home; in fact we have a stammered pot picked out, by the main road where all the trees are gathered."

I spluttered out so excited to have my brother and his family close to us and a boy, to carry on the family name.

Even with the truth that James found out he decided that it didn't matter, that our father had loved him as his son and that is just the way it should be.

We had opened the inn back up and with the rooms we saved for James, Kelly and the girls, we were full.

Our dinner table had interesting guests to trill us and family around to keep us grounded.

The rooms all fresh and painted with the grand antique furniture we found along with the old lace curtains and old and new quilts on the beds, the rooms were quit comfortable to stay in and enjoy.

We hung a quilting frame up in the main front room and spent Wednesday nights teaching quilting to the town younger woman and our guests. The twins took to it with grandma teaching them all the tricks.

Mother loved having all her granddaughters close and was really looking forward to a grandson soon.

May came in with nights filled with rain and days filled with sunshine. It was perfect for James, jack and Bob to hire workers to build a starter home for James and his family. They put in a huge fenced yard to keep the kids in and a huge porch for them to sit and watch the world pass by.

The house sat back from the road surrounded by huge trees, that dad had left to grow for years. It was a really nice spot for a home and we always knew that was dad's plan to have one or both of his children move back home to live the simple wonderful life of living off the land, to grow your own food, to help your neighbors thru the hard times with expecting to be paid back.

The neighbors we helped out each winter came to help us after they worked all day on their farm. It took three weeks for James and Kelly to move in with the girls sharing a room for now. They had plans laid out to add two bedrooms off the back of the house for the girls to each have there own room and the new baby a room.

Jack planted the crops during his days and helped out until late at night, Belle and I would see him coming and going, but we understood and we were busy ourselves. There was more work then people at the inn to do the work, meals to be cook, beds to be made and floors to be vacuumed daily.

With the inn and farm paying for it selves we decided to use my inheritance for good elsewhere.

We had always given to the church in town and even got James, Kelly and the twins to start attending with us every Sunday.

We gave to the town for the repair of the cemetery and park at the school. We even paid for the library to be updated as well.

We built a senior center and put Bob and mom in charge of it and offered free heath care for the seniors that lived in town and any one else who walked in.

We built a childcare business in town for the children with a state of the art play area and the best care that money could pay for.

Jack, mother and I had the most fun coming up with ideals to help out with the money we got each month.

With all the fun, and family around, Jack and I decided it was time to give Belle a younger sister or brother to play with.

At first it upset me that there would be talk that we had a baby just to get more money but we decided that with all the good we did for the town there would be less bad talk and more good and besides as Jack pointed out to me, those who love us and know us know the truth and the rest can go to hell.

Laughing as he said it because I scoffed at him for cussing around Belle. She was still sleeping in our room.

It was hard to fine time to ourselves to make a baby much less say hello to each other but we did the best we could and by the end of June, I was expecting too.

Kelly's baby was due in December and mine three months later in March, Belle would turn three the next month after my birth, so it was perfect timing.

So we turned mothers room in to a child bedroom for Belle, for now and the new baby too, later.

We just couldn't put Belle back across the hallway in James old room.

We put in a rest stop off the main freeway that ran thru town and named it in horror of dad, he would have loved it.

With the twins around belle had someone to play with and she just loved each girl, even knowing which twin was which, and we still had trouble telling them apart sometimes. We would call one of the girls by the wrong name and Belle would laugh and tell us different. It was a really fun time for all of us enjoying each others company.

Summer came and went in such a furry that it was hard to believe it had gone so fast. The guests filled the rooms up fast as we could clean them from the last guests.

Kelly helped me with some of the lighter chores while James opened up a second hand shop in town that was doing very well.

He filled the shop with antiques, old lace, candles sticks, a hundred years old and fine china from around the world, that we would find in small shops and large shops that had estate sales.

We would leave the girls at home with mother and Bob for the weekend and the four of us would go on hunts thru the country towns and some big city shops to hunt for old stuff to fill our inn and James new shop.

In fact that was how James came up with the ideal for the shop on our leftovers from our hunts.

Our guests would hit the store on the way out of town and some as they arrived looking for deals to take home to remind them of our home. The inn.

James got real good at wrapping small and large breakables for shipping or traveling.

As we moved into fall, the ghosts starting acting up again, driving the guests and us crazy. The guests loved all the spooky happenings.

We didn't care for the noise at night and moved Belles bed into our bedroom, even thou the guests were asked to stay over in the right side of the house; we would hear them in the halls late at night chasing the ghosts.

The lights would flicker off and on late at night with out a single time it happening during the day.

It was spooky, to say the least. Most of the guests would call it a show and say we set it up but we knew the truth and sense we had returned it seemed to be getting worse.

Some times it would be quieter then other nights where the whole house be woken by the noise.

The ghosts was getting out of hand but until Halloween night no one had been hurt by the ghosts or because of them.

What happened that night left us scared for good. The guests that stayed that night got more then they paid for, and we charged big to stay at the inn on Halloween night, it was booked in advance for months ahead.

We decorated it all out with orange and black with witch's and spiders.

The girls love helping us decorator it up for the night. We never counted on the ghosts to make it quiet so scary, but they I guess wanted to make a showing for us and our guests that stayed that night at the inn.

The guests had no idea of the severity the situation but Jack and I did.

We knew that we would have to have someone help us with our haunted inn, until that night it was fun and games with no one hurt. And the ghosts that seemed to haunt our inn up until that night had been friendly ghosts.

That night the ghosts that came to play had the look and feel of pure evil, like the devil himself.

Chapter 20
"The Homecoming"
By Deana Rae Higgins

Fun with ghosts

My home had been invaded by object's moving, door's slamming, light's flickering, footsteps in the hall, ghosts.

We needed help and we needed it fast, I called everyone I could think of and finically went to the internet for help. I found someone to come and visit us, on their first visit they found proof that there was indeed a ghost in our home. So they wanted to hold a ghost hunt on Halloween, and wanted us to empty the inn, but Jack wouldn't hear of it, after what happened that night, I wished we had listened to them.

Halloween started like any other rainy day, dark, and running late. It was spooky from the start; there was even a dense fog that morning that hung around long after the rain stopped.

We spent the day setting up Halloween decorations.

"Jack, please can't we talk about what they said, I have this feeling that something's going to happen, please Jack." I pleaded.

"NO Cara-Ann, its just a scam, I don't buy this ghost crap like you do, no its our best paying day at the inn and we are no turning them away for some ghost hunt." Jack barked back at me.

"Jack we don't need the money, I have…" I started to say but was rudely cut off by Jack.

"That's it Cara-Ann, your money, your farm, yours, what's mine, huh, I work hard around here to earn MY way and you want to skip it and live off your money, no. Hell NO!"

"I don't want to talk about this subject, its closed you understand, now if you'll EXCUSE me I have work to do, not all of can be daddy's little girl and live like a princess, la tee daa." And he stormed off, leaving me standing with my mouth hanging open.

I had never heard Jack talk to anyone, not even his workers, the way he had just talked to me, I really was scared now, it was this house, I just knew it.

I called Carol the medium who had visited the farm

to do the tests, I had saved a room for them, just in case I needed it, and I felt I did, so I invited them to come stay the night with us and help us make it thru Halloween night alive.

They set up the stuff around the farm without Jack seeing them until dinner when we all sat down together to eat. I had made turkey with all the fixings, James, Kelly and the girls came over too from there new house up the street, mother and Bob stayed home to go to bed early.

Boy was I glad they had, wish I had.

Before we could even get started on dinner the lights went out and we needed to light the candles, and thru out dinner one or two would blow out with a unfelt breeze that would blow them out.

When the table started lifting, first on one side then the other side before the whole table lifted up several feet from the floor.

We all pushed our chairs back in fear, but then everyone but Jack, me and Carol's crew, started laughing out loud, thinking it was a set up by us, it wasn't.

We finished dinner with the table suspended in mid air. We had to stand and everyone thought this was a great ideal. A standing restaurant

After dinner we all went into the setting area for a

night cape. We had had a late dinner for the children to go treat or treating, all three girls dressed in matching angel outfits, I had made, maybe to bring us luck, it didn‘t work..

We sent the children upstairs to bed, the twins sleeping in Belle’s room with her, they were so tired from walking around town, that they fell asleep before there heads hit the bed, they slept all night not waking, even thru the noise, thou I couldn‘t figure out how.

As soon as we settled in, the objects in the room, started to fly around, soft as butterflies floating by on a nice spring afternoon.

Everyone was in total awe watching small what knot’s float in slow dance like moves, even jumping up and dancing, following the cups, glass animal’s we had collected, and small lace dollies, laughing as they danced.

When they started to speed up and slammed in to the fireplace, like something from an old movie, they still laughed, wanting to pay ahead for next years Halloween night..

By this time Jack was glad that Carol and her bunch had been called in to stay the night, I know I was glad I had called.

It took about three seconds for things to turn ugly and very scary. The breakables started flying around a circle faster and faster, so fast we all sit down back on the couch's, love seats and chairs in the room around the fireplace.

The glass became a wall of glass flying in a tornado in the middle of the room, in front of the fireplace. You could hear the braking as all of the objects hit each other joining into a swirling mass of glass in front of our eyes.

I saw the danger and yelled to everyone to close their eyes just as the tornado exposed in air and flew outward in directional outward waves, hitting everyone in the room at the same time, like a glass bomb.

The guests didn't fare well and all of them left, right then, either to the hospital, with glass in their eyes or in fear for there lives.

Carol wanted all of us to leave but James and I screamed out no way tighter, making our spouses stay too.

It was our home that we had grown up on and we couldn't leave even if we wanted, dads sprit had made himself know to us both, and we felt it was what dad wanted, us to stay and fight the demons who held our home hostage.

Besides I felt I knew where the hate and evil that had joined our home was coming from. The Blacks had found a way to stay and hunt us, maybe it was the love of a daughter that held Jason and his brothers here.

Or the hate of losing their lives so young because of me and Jack, and Belle. But it was time for them to leave.

A showdown over my sweet Annabelle. I was ready to face whatever I had to, the guys begged me and Kelly to leave after we were pregnant but we wouldn't have it plus somehow being with child made us feel stronger to fight evil, like we held gods angles, touched by everything good and loving, in our womb.

We stood our grown and waited for the show to start again, it had taken an hour to clear the farm and nothing had happened during that time.

As soon as we sat down, things started lifting, the candles all blew out leaving us in the dark, but we had been prepared with flash lights in hand.

In the light of our flashlights, soft white clear forms took shape, some with no leg's, just a skirt flapping in the wind made by them flying around the room.

It was the Black brothers, I could hear the laughter made by them, as they flew faster and faster around the room. Jason seemed to be the brightest and in charge of the rest, there were more forms then the Blacks so they must have recruited in hell.

You could feel the evil that came from the swirl of white that surrounded the room.

Carol stood and tried to yell some words to the evil sprits that moved over our heads. But a huge hand came out, like something drawn in a cartoon and pushed her hard back down into the couch she had been on before.

The swirl was so strong that non of us could move, our hands plastered down to our sides as if weighted down by a unseen force field.

The air around took on a horrible smell, like death. All of us started gagging, the smell so bad that I noticed that Kelly had vomited on her blouse, running slowly down the front, like it was held by force.

Then it stopped and we all jumped up out of our chairs. We walked the house checking on the girls and sending Kelly to bed with them.

The only room that seemed to be affected was the setting room, the place that Jason would wait for me when we dated back in school.

Carol set about laying some books out on the coffee table, a cross and some holly water. Her crew set up camera's and recording machines to catch everything on tape.

Jack, James and I set down on the couch to watch as Carol started trying to clear our farm of evil sprits.

As soon as she started praying the ghosts started up

again, I looked around and there were ghosts everywhere just standing around watching what Carol was doing.

There was a old cop standing by the door, in his forties uniform, there was a boy with a big black lap by his side, who wave at me, I waved back, making Jack frown, as he couldn't see what I was seeing.

An older lady was sitting in a chair mending socks. They seemed to be in all kinds of dress from the early days to modern days. Ladies with long dress and girls in mini skirts standing together.

Men in kinds of uniforms from older southern blues to firemen and police officers, even spacesuits, just standing to the side watching.

Suddenly from out of no where a huge white spiral ghost with no form just a soft cloud, pushed carol very hard for the side, pushing her to the floor.

Jack saw nothing hit her but when she fell, he ran to help her up and was shoved to the floor as well. He lay there with Carol, both upset and frightened but unharmed.

The force that had knocked them to the floor knocked the wind out of both off them. The air grew cold around me as I blended into the back of the couch, held there by a strong unseen ropes.

Everything got eerie quite around us, all the ghosts moved to the walls and turned to the fireplace, they pointed and there mouths fell open wider then a live person could ever open there mouth, and a high shrill flew out in high pitched screams.

From the fireplace a black smelly smoke began to descend out from the chimney opening. It was evil and as it came out it began to form life forms that started as dust and slowly became clearer.

As the black, dusty, ashes, formed, it became clear it was three men, or ghosts of three men, and in no time I knew it was the Black brothers.

I screamed in horror, as jack and Carol raced back to where I was sitting. I realized I could move and jumped from my seat screaming along with the ghosts that stood along the wall.

Evil was descending from hell in the from of the Blacks brothers.
I could not believe what was happening in front of my eyes. Jack and Carol where having trouble believing it too, yet we all saw this part, including Jack who up till now had no sight of the ghosts.

Jack looked around the room in fear and awe as he now saw all the other ghosts surrounding us.

The other ghosts began to shrink back into the

walls in fear as the brothers took shape. They still screamed in fear and I wanted to join them as they passed thru the walls. The sight before me scared me as no other sight had ever done so. Jack and Carol had a look of fear on there face too, the camera and sound men that where with Carol had moved as far back as the could without losing picture or sound.

As the brothers formed they began to laugh a horrible evil laugh.

"I've come back for my sweet Cara-Ann, and to watch you die Jackie, my boy. My brothers want to have a little talk with you. There not in a very good mood, ever since you killed them, my boy, they been a bit cranky, but we do love this new form the devil himself gave us." Jason the first to form in front yelled as he turned from see thru to a solid mass, unlike the other ghosts who had a clearness about them.

We could not move and we could not open our mouths, we seemed to be paralyzed by a unseen force. As we sat there watching the brothers become solid and strong, we watched, in horror, there was nothing we could do to stop them from doing what ever they wanted to do to us, even the camera guys and sound guys seemed to be unable to move but still held the camera's to capture all that was forming in front of our eyes. It was if the brothers wanted the world to see them in all there glory of evilness.

As they moved, they appeared to float on air, I just knew that all of us would die right there and then.

The air changed and all the ghosts shut up at the same time. When the black brothers entered the air grew hot and hard to breath like all the oxygen had been sucked out of the room.

The more formed they became the harder it was to breath at all.
All of us gasped for air as we watched.

The Black brothers moved as if they owned the air, there was a powerful force to them that was super strong as well as evil.

We all tried to moved to scream to even breath but we could do nothing but stare in fear as we slowly suffocated to death.

The air grew colder with a sweet smell like fresh snow, we all took a deep breath, sucking in as fast as we could. The look on the black brothers turned from evil and hateful to confused. We all looked to see what it was they saw that changed and saw Belle.

She stood at the door and light stood all around her as if she was the center of the moon, or a star or even the sun.

She had on her white nightgown that lit up like a

captured star. Above her head a white ring seemed to light up her back and hair.

She entered the room and all the ghosts smiled as she pass them, like being close to Belle was the same as a movie star or maybe a saint of some sort. Belle didn't run or even seem to be afraid of the situation that was going on. She held her arms out as if she was hugging the whole world and had this smile on her face that lit up the room as she moved to the center of the room.

She passed us all as she made her way to the front of the Black brothers. All of us tried to stop her, reach out and catch her but the other ghosts all started shaking there heads no, that there was no need to stop her, yet we tried and couldn't reach thru the white cloud that protected her, surrounding her.

She stop in front of the brothers who stood there spell bound by the sight of Belle and her light. A smiled formed on all three faces of the brothers as she stopped in front of them. She held out her hand touching all three as she did and suddenly the black started to turn to white. The whiteness moved thru the blackness of the Black brothers with fine bright lines that flowed into the mass of evil.

As it flowed like blood thru veins it turned everything it touched to white. A high scream that had no form yet had a sense of being alive seemed to be fleeing in fear and pain, pulling away from the Black brothers as if one would run from fire. The evil held on and didn't want to let go but the power in Belle was stronger then the evil.

And just like that it let go and drifted back into the fireplace like a back wards movie. The Black brothers turned from gray ash into a soft white color. They held there hands outstretched to Belle's out stretched hand and the whiteness that surrounded Belle over took the brothers as well in gulf all of them in a bright white cloud, and then they all three turned to dust that sprinkled the floor like snowflakes falling. It was beautiful to watch.

With out missing a beat, Belle turned to her dad Jack and asked for a bedtime story. She felt no fear and looked as if she didn't know what had just happened and she never remembered so we never told her about the night she became an angel from heaven and send the evil back to hell.

Carol wrote a book and sold the movie rights for a movie but she never told where the farm was located or our real names so no one knew it was Belle.

We kept the inn running and the friendly ghosts stayed and haunted it on a nightly basis, it was rented out every night and kept us all very busy.

About two months later Jack and I went to have an

ultrasound done and we're expecting twins, both boys, so the family will have three boys added.

Mom, Bob, James, Kelly and the girls came over for dinner, it had been three years sense I came home, it was nothing like what I thought it would be like, it was better.

P.S. Letter from dad…

Dear Belle,

Years ago, my father dug up the treasure box and opened a safety deposit box at the bank for me…

Forgive me for making you think it was still hidden under the old tree, but I needed to protect the contents and it was easier to protect the tree…

Guess I got one over good on your uncle, the mayor…

If your reading this, I've gone on, please take care of your mother, brother and yourself for me, I love you, your mother and James very much, please ask James jr. to forgive me, I couldn't tell him, I always thought of him as my son.

In love,
Father

ISBN 978-0-6151-4923-3

All names and or places come from writer's mind, Made up by writer.

higginsdeana@hotmail.com

www.ingramcontent.com/pod-product-compliance
Lightning Source LLC
Chambersburg PA
CBHW020613310726
48979CB00008B/1469/J

* 9 7 8 0 6 1 5 1 4 9 2 3 3 *